Young Dedalus
General Editor: Timothy La

# MEMOIRS
# OF A
# BASQUE COW

15940

*Bernardo Atxaga*

# MEMOIRS
# OF A
# BASQUE COW

translated by Margaret Jull Costa

Dedalus

The translation of this work was supported by a grant from the Etxepare Basque Institute.

Published in the UK by Dedalus Limited
24-26, St Judith's Lane, Sawtry, Cambs, PE28 5XE
info@dedalusbooks.com
www.dedalusbooks.com

ISBN printed book   978 1 912868 01 8
ISBN ebook   978 1 912868 27 8

Dedalus is distributed in the USA & Canada by SCB Distributors
15608 South New Century Drive, Gardena, CA 90248
info@scbdistributors.com   www.scbdistributors.com

Dedalus is distributed in Australia by Peribo Pty Ltd
58, Beaumont Road, Mount Kuring-gai, N.S.W. 2080
info@peribo.com.au

First published by Dedalus in 2020
*Behi Euskaldun Baten Memoriak* © *1992 Bernardo Atxaga*
*This book was negotiated through Ute Körner Lterary Agent - www.uklitag.com*
*Translation* © *Margaret Jull Costa 2020*

Printed and bound in Great Britain by Clays, Elcograf S.p.A
Typeset by Marie Lane

A C.I.P. listing for this book is available on request.

# THE AUTHOR

Bernardo Atxaga (born 1950) is considered to be the finest Basque writer of his generation. He has written novels, short stories, song lyrics, plays and children's literature. His books have been translated into more than twenty languages, and his work in euskera (Basque) and in translation has brought him many prizes, including the Premio Nacional de Narrativa, the Premio Euskadi, the Premio de la Crítica, the Prix Millepages, the Premio Valle-Inclán, and the Marsh Award for Children's Literature in Translation.

# THE TRANSLATOR

Margaret Jull Costa has translated the works of many Spanish and Portuguese writers. She won the Portuguese Translation Prize for *The Book of Disquiet* by Fernando Pessoa in 1992 and for *The Word Tree* by Teolinda Gersão in 2012, and her translations of Eça de Queiroz's novels *The Relic* (1996) and *The City and the Mountains* (2009) were shortlisted for the prize; with Javier Marías, she won the 1997 International IMPAC Dublin Literary Award for *A Heart So White*, and, in 2000, she won the Oxford Weidenfeld Translation Prize for José Saramago's *All the Names*. In 2008 she won the Pen Book-of-the Month-Club Translation Prize and the Oxford Weidenfeld Translation Prize for *The Maias* by Eça de Queiroz.

# PREFACE

One day, while on a walk through some woods up in the mountains in the Basque Country, I met with two surprises. The first was seeing a newborn calf, its eyes still tight shut, lying on the grass; the second, shortly afterwards, was finding the rusting remains of what, at first sight, appeared to be a small plane. I pondered the fate of both. What would become of the calf when she became a cow? What was the story behind that plane?

The second question was rather easier to answer. I was helped by a mechanic who went with me to the place where I'd found what was now just a jumble of engine parts and bits of fuselage.

'It's definitely a war plane,' he said, pointing to a couple of lumps of metal, 'because those would have been the machine guns.' He was an older, rather serious man.

'I suppose it must date from the 1936 war,' I said.

'Indeed,' he answered. 'We've never had another

war like that here. Well, years ago, of course, there were wars involving cavalry, but not airplanes.'

The history books explain what happened in Spain in 1936. General Franco rose up against the legitimate Republican government, and that uprising provoked a civil war, a bloodbath that went on for nearly three years, from 1936 to 1939. Thanks, in part, to support from Nazi Germany and Fascist Italy, Franco's troops won, and General Franco then imposed a dictatorship that lasted for forty years, until 1975. The remains I'd stumbled upon in the woods in the mountains were a memento from that civil war.

The mechanic and I inspected what was left of the wings. I wanted to find out the name of the manufacturer and the plane's country of origin, but there was no way of telling. The rust had eaten away any emblems or lettering.

'The war was a truly terrible thing,' said the mechanic, looking around him at the trees in the wood. 'But the years that followed weren't exactly good either. There were even groups of resistance fighters living in these very mountains.'

He was referring to the anti-fascist rebels who fled into the mountains after the war and tried to face down the Franco dictatorship. This surprised me. I'd heard about such rebels living in other parts of the country, in the Serranía de Cuenca and in the Picos de Europa, but not in the Basque Country.

'They were fewer in number, but they were definitely here,' said the mechanic.

# PREFACE

Having found an answer to my question about the plane, I then started thinking about the life of cows. Not the future life of the newborn calf I'd come across in the woods, but the lives of the cows who had lived through the post-war years in those same mountains, alongside resistance fighters on the run from Franco's Civil Guard. There was no easy answer to this. Who knows what mysteries might lie hidden behind a cow's eyes? What does a cow see? And how much does she understand of what she sees? Everything? A small part? Nothing?

In the end, I felt I had come up with one possible answer. I was helped by logic, but, more than anything, by my imagination. The result is this book which you, dear reader, now hold in your hands, the story of a cow named Mo.

Bernardo Atxaga

# First Chapter

What my inner voice ordered me to do, or how I
came to the decision to write these bovine memoirs.
I recall what happened one very snowy night.

It was a night of thunder and lightning, and the noise and the racket made by the storm finally woke me from my sleep.

Then my inner voice said: 'Listen, my dear, has not the hour arrived? Is this not the appropriate, correct and most suitable moment?' And not long afterwards, without even giving me time to wake up properly: 'Should you not abandon sleep and comfort? Should you not embrace the excellent, fruitful light? Tell me briefly and with your hand on your heart, has not the hour arrived? Is not this the appropriate, correct and convenient moment?'

This inner voice of mine has a very prissy, formal way of speaking, and seems incapable of talking like everyone else and simply calling grass 'grass' and straw 'straw'; if she had her way, instead of grass, we would say: 'the wholesome food grown for us by Mother Earth' and instead of straw: 'the unwholesome alternative that one must eat when good food is in short supply'. The voice I hear inside me always speaks like that, which means that she takes an incredibly long time to explain anything, which means that most of what she has to say is very boring, which means that in order to listen to her without screaming, you have to be extremely patient. Even if you did scream, it wouldn't make any difference, because she won't go away, she's not going to just disappear.

When I was still young, a cow of a certain age called Bidani once said to me: 'She can't disappear, because she's our Guardian Angel. You should be glad to know that she's there inside you. In this life she will be your very best friend, and will always comfort you when you feel alone. If you find yourself with a difficult choice to make, just listen to your inner voice, and she'll tell you which is the best choice to make. If you find yourself in grave danger, never fear, just place your life in the hands of your Guardian Angel and she will guide your steps.'

'Am I supposed to believe that?' I asked Bidani.

'Of course,' she replied rather arrogantly.

'Well, I'm sorry, but I don't believe a word of it.'

What else could I say? She was older than me, there was no doubt about that, but compared to me, she was also extremely gullible. The fact is that the person has not yet been born who can explain to me exactly what a Guardian Angel is, and so I choose not to believe it. That's the way I am. When something is clearly true, when, for example, someone puts a pile of fenugreek in front of me and says: 'This is fenugreek,' then I go over and I smell it and I say: 'Yes, this is fenugreek.' I recognise that what they say is true, but if there's no proof, or if the proof doesn't even smell, then I choose not to believe. As the saying goes:

> WHAT DID YOU THINK LIFE WAS ALL
> ABOUT — BELIEVING EVERYTHING
> YOU'RE TOLD AND NEVER
> EXPRESSING A DOUBT?

No, sir, that's not living, that's just playing the fool and behaving no better than a sheep.

'You don't understand, my dear,' insisted Bidani, as arrogantly as ever. 'Your Guardian Angel can't possibly smell of anything. She's an angel and lives inside us like a spirit; she doesn't take up any room at all.'

'You should have been a sheep,' I said with all the impudence I could muster; then, turning my back on her, I stalked off.

Whatever the truth of the matter, though, and

regardless of whether I believed it or not, that inner voice was always there, and I had to accept her. It made no difference what you called her — Guardian Angel, Spirit, Voice or Conscience — she was always there inside me.

One day, I asked the voice: 'What's your name?' At that time, I spoke to her respectfully, for I was very young.

'Whatever you like, my dear. As far as I'm concerned, I am entirely in your hands, I'm your servant. And, let me just say, I accept my servitude gladly.'

'Yes, I'm sure, but just tell me, please, what's your name?'

'I'm sorry, my dear, but, as I have just explained, I am entirely at your disposal. It is up to the mistress to name her servant.'

I got annoyed then and said: 'Oh, you are a pest! You're the very peskiest of pests. I don't know whether you're an angel or an evil spirit, I don't know what you're doing inside me either, but I know exactly the kind of person you are, I should say I do. You're the kind who always has to have her own way.'

Then, nursing the little bit of anger I felt, I made a decision: I would call that supposed Guardian

Angel 'The Pest'. And ever since then, that is precisely what she has been: The Pest, The Pesky Pest.

'Well, I can't say it's the nicest name I've ever encountered,' I heard the voice say, 'but it could be worse.'

That said, and despite everything, I didn't really think that badly of my inner pest; I couldn't honestly disagree with all those who spoke in her favour. Sometimes she did seem like my best friend, a good companion when life was pleasant and an even better one when life turned sour, and when she spoke to me, I listened gladly. Indeed, I remember what happened during my very first winter. Then she was a true companion, then she really did behave like a real friend. It all happened one snowy day.

'Look, my dear, it's snowing,' the voice inside me said. 'It's started to snow and we're quite far from the house. It might be a good idea to begin making your way down the hill.'

'Down the hill? You must be joking!' I said bluntly. It was the first time I had ever seen snow, and I didn't understand how dangerous those snowflakes melting on my back could be. So I again turned my attention to eating grass, because, it has to be said, I can't resist that short, succulent hilltop grass; I've never been satisfied with boring field grass.

I'm not sure how long I spent there nibbling the short grass, without even once looking up, but I don't think it could have been very long — maybe half an hour, maybe an hour. Nevertheless, because of the snow that had fallen, it was soon impossible for me to go on eating. I stretched out my lips in search of more grass, but all I got was a mouthful of snow. I snuffled the ground as I'd seen pigs do, and all I got was another chilly lump of snow. Irritated, I raised my head and looked around me. Then I really did feel afraid. And who could blame me, given what I saw.

There was a black rock, a lot of snow, and nothing else. The meadow where I'd been grazing was white, and the next one was white too, and all the others were white as well. And the path that crossed them to go down to my house was nowhere to be seen; it had disappeared beneath all that whiteness.

'What's going on here? How will I ever get home now?' I said to myself, taking a few steps towards the black rock. I felt quite worried.

I mooed to see if some companion would reply

and guide me back to the homeward path, but the silence swallowed my voice the way a frog swallows a fly, and my calls for help simply disappeared. There was nothing but the silence, the whiteness of the snow and the blackness of the rock. And The Pest didn't say a word. She was obviously hurt by my earlier rude reply.

The whiteness was just as white when the first star appeared, and when the second star appeared too. And when the third, the fourth and the fifth appeared, it was still the same. Then it was the moon's turn, and that did change things slightly, by adding a few shadows to the landscape. Nothing very much though. The whiteness covered almost everything. And there I was. As the saying goes:

A HILLSIDE UNDER SNOW MAKES
FOR AN UNHAPPY COW.

I was that cow and I was very unhappy. Where was the path home? Would it never come back? It certainly didn't look like it.

'Well, have you got nothing to say to me, Pest?' I said at last. I really had to do something to get myself out of that situation. If I didn't, I might simply die of boredom.

'I'm going to say something, but it won't be what you want to hear.'

The voice was obviously angry, because she didn't even call me 'my dear'. Now that I think of it, The Pest must have been very young in those days too; otherwise, she wouldn't have got so angry over one cheeky reply. I say worse things to her now, and she takes no notice. Now, of course, I always obey in the end and do what she wants me to do.

'Go on, then. I'm so fed up, I'll listen to anything,' I replied.

'You owe me an apology. When the snow started falling and I suggested that you should go home, there was no reason why you should obey me. You're a free agent and you can do what you like, but, my dear, you had no right to reply in that rude, vulgar, ill-bred fashion. You had absolutely no right to do that, my dear. Manners come first, above all else.'

I looked to the left and to the right, I looked to one side of the black rock, I looked to the other, I looked everywhere, and there wasn't a sign of the path. The hill was either white with snow or black with night, with nothing in between. I was very bored and very fed up.

'I'm sorry,' I said at last.

'You're forgiven, of course,' said The Pest, with very good grace, forgetting her annoyance. Then

20

she added with a sigh: 'Just look where we are!'

'Where?' I said, cheering up. That was exactly what I wanted to know, where I was and how I could get home, but The Pest was talking about something else.

'We're in a desert, my dear. That's how I would describe it; a white desert has fallen out of the sky, bit by bit. What solitude! What desolation! Here one truly feels how very small and feeble one is!'

'I'm a cow, what do you expect! What can you expect from cows! We cows are nothing,' I exclaimed in a fit of honesty. Because, frankly, I've never thought being a cow was anything very special. The way I look at it, we cows pass through this world almost unnoticed, along the vulgar path of mediocrity, and to tell the truth and, sad though it may seem, the creature we most resemble is the sheep. As the saying goes:

WHAT'S THE DIFFERENCE BETWEEN A
COW AND A SHEEP?
ONE'S LAZY, THE OTHER'S WEAK.

Of course The Pest doesn't think like that, she thinks there's something rather grand about cows, and that the rest of the animal kingdom is a bit beneath us. She naturally disagreed with my view and then — what with the snow and the solitude created by the snow — she composed a kind of hymn of praise to our race.

'You're wrong to talk about cows in that way, and you shouldn't run yourself down,' she said.

'Maybe,' I said, prudently.

'Of course you shouldn't, my dear. A cow isn't just anything. Consider, for example, what is happening here. Who is here in this frozen desert, in the midst of this great solitude? Only you, my dear. Or to put it another way, the cow is here. The cow and not, for example, the mole. In autumn, yes, in the warmth of autumn, the moles would be toiling away here and there and frolicking about, but where are they now? And what about the worms and the ants and all the other creatures? They're nowhere, because they have run away; they have fled under the earth, burrowing deeper and ever deeper; and who knows where those cowards are now, possibly at the very centre of the earth. And what can one say about those who walked, or rather slithered, among the grasses — snakes and serpents of every kind? Or the lizards who peered out of the cracks in the rocks? They've all run away and are now sleeping in some hidey-hole. Even more superior creatures have fled — the birds, for example, the squirrels and the pigs and the chickens. Yes, my dear, they have all run away, every one of them, and only you, the cow, remain. A cow understands about solitude and desolation, and armed with that knowledge, can face up to life. Being a cow is really quite magnificent!'

'Well, I certainly wouldn't disagree with you there,' I said, looking at the black rock in front of me. It seemed to me that The Pest was right in a way; the ability simply to be there quietly, fearlessly, was no mean feat.

Nevertheless, fear is one thing, boredom's quite another, and whilst I might be able to face up to the former, the latter was not the same thing at all. I was getting tired of that icy place, and time was beginning to drag — and drag. When would dawn come? When would daylight show me the way home? But it was no use, I had better just resign myself. It probably wasn't even midnight yet; the moon and the stars had been out for some time. In the end, and most reluctantly, because it wounded my pride, I resorted to the only company I had to hand.

'Tell me, Pest, how are we going to get out of here?' I said.

'I'm sorry, my dear, but I can't tell you everything. If I told you everything, you would never learn to think for yourself, and you would become as simple a creature as a sheep. Why don't you just apply your mind to the problem, my dear? If you did that, you would find the way home in no time.'

If I hadn't been in such an awkward situation, something might have occurred to me, but it was a very awkward situation indeed and getting worse by the minute. I made an effort to see how I had got there, where the house was, what the path looked like, but I felt as if I had a great slab sitting on my mind, crushing any answers.

'Can't you give me a clue, my friend?' I said then, and I don't know how I could bring myself to say that, calling The Pest 'my friend', buttering her up. I was very young, of course, and I was fed up with being stranded on that hill. But those are just excuses; the fact is that I demeaned myself. There are no two ways about it, the truth is that now, if I could, I would kick myself hard in that part of one's anatomy one doesn't usually mention. Worse, The Pest was not even prepared to give in.

'No, I told you "no". You must give that head of yours a good shake and set it to work. It's dark, that's true, and the snow has erased all the roads and paths, but that shouldn't be a problem for someone with the power to think. Think, my dear, and you will soon be home.'

'Thanks for nothing,' I said as coarsely as I could and, grim-faced, I lay down in the snow and stared at the black rock. After a while, I half turned round and stared in the other direction. In that position, though, I couldn't even see the rock, and I decided to turn round again. Although it was cold, my whole body was burning. I thought: 'I'll get up and empty my bowels. Perhaps that will distract me.'

But it was no good. I didn't feel like it. And I had no alternative but to continue being bored. In the end, I just stretched out my neck and bellowed with all my might: 'What's going on here! What's happening, why aren't I frightened? If I was frightened, I wouldn't be so bored!'

'Now that's what I call bellowing, my dear,' exclaimed my Inner Voice. 'And would you believe it, that bellowing of yours might just resolve your problem, since it will have alerted the local pack of wolves to the fact that you're here; they're very hungry wolves, by the way, and they'd love to gobble up a nice tender little creature like you. I wouldn't be at all surprised if they didn't arrive this instant. They're probably on their way right now. Of course, I know how brave you are and that a wolf or two or even three would be nothing to you. Just deal them a couple of kicks each and that'll be that. But a whole pack of wolves, about sixteen of them, that's another matter. I don't know, it's up to you, but I think I'd probably leave — fast, quickly, at the double, in a word, pronto.'

What did The Pest mean? What was all that about wolves? Wolves? Hungry wolves? Sixteen wolves? What did The Pest mean, 'sixteen wolves'? Where had all those wolves suddenly sprung from? A shiver ran down my spine, but I decided to stand firm and stay where I was. My pride as a cow left me no alternative.

'Be quiet, Pest!' I said. 'What do you mean "wolves"? This is the twentieth century, you know! Only a fool would believe such a thing!'

'Of course, my dear, this is the twentieth century, or, to be more exact, 1940, but we are in the Basque Country, and in the Basque Country there's been a war going on until recently, the Civil War of 1936, and there's a lot of hunger, a lot of poverty, not enough people to clear the woods, and rumour has it that the woods are full of wolves.'

'Well, there might be rumours flying around, but no wolves,' I said to The Pest, trying to make a joke of it, but my tail was still twitching. Wolves!

Sixteen wolves! Sixteen hungry wolves! And me a mere cow. Not just any cow, but a cow all the same.

Suddenly, on the surface of the black rock, a shape appeared, a black shape, like a lump. Up until only a short time before, there had been nothing but a lot of snow and a black rock, now there was a lot of snow, a black rock and a lump. After a while, two more black lumps appeared: a lot of snow, a black rock and three lumps, four lumps, six lumps, nine lumps.

'What's more they've all got ears,' I thought, looking harder. I leapt to my feet.

'Rotten wolves! A whole gang of them too! Come at me one at a time and then we'll see what's what!' I said, or rather I didn't, I just imagined that I did.

'My dear, think a little,' said The Pest. 'Where is your house? Where can it be?'

Just at that moment, when my tail was beginning to tremble, light dawned. I was on the top of a hill, wasn't I? I was up the hill. Therefore, what was the solution?

'To go down!' I said to myself. Besides, it was possible that there might not be any snow lower down and the path would be clear. Bracing myself from head to foot, I set off at a trot. By then, the black rock was covered in lumps, at least sixteen of them, all with ears.

'Wait, my dear,' said The Pest at that moment, and just at the right moment, like a real friend. 'I know that back home in the barn no one can beat you at running, but one of those wolves probably could. Don't trot, just take it slowly and calmly, as if you were looking for the odd blade of grass to eat. That way they won't attack immediately. They'll follow you, but they won't attack. You must keep a cool head, my dear.'

Realising that The Pest was right, I began to move nonchalantly. I took three steps and stopped. I waited a little, then took another two steps. Three steps, four steps, two steps. I looked out of the corner of my eye at the rock: all the lumps were now on the snow, and there were sixteen of them, all with ears. I took a step, the ones with the ears took another. I took three, they took three. Ahead of me lay only the darkness of the night and the whiteness of the snow, and some stars and a moon. At one point, a kind of spasm ran through my tail, and I forgot myself and took five rather rapid steps.

'Careful, my friend,' I heard the voice say inside me. All the lumps were bunched together only a few yards from me; I could hear them breathing.

Boldly, without thinking twice, I turned round to face the wolves and I started calmly and contentedly eating the snow, as if it wasn't snow before me, but whole bunches of fenugreek. When they saw this, the lumps seemed disconcerted and stopped in their tracks, first one, and then the others. I noticed that apart from ears they also had eyes: pointed ears and reddish eyes. Then, without losing my composure, I started to retreat, quite fast, one two three, one two three, one two three, and the wolves, one two three, didn't take their eyes off me, but, one two three, they still couldn't quite decide to attack. And thus, one two three, one two three, we reached a grove of trees. I remembered that grove of trees; it was just above my house.

'Beyond the trees there's a steep slope, and at the end of the slope is the path home,' I thought. 'If, when I get there, I hurl myself down the hill, I might break a leg, but at least those wolves won't get me.'

'A great idea!' I heard the voice say inside me.

I again began to advance, little by little, watching the sixteen wolves out of the corner of my eye. They still had ears and eyes, but, worse, they had mouths. They had red mouths and white teeth. From time to time, one of them would start howling, and behind him the others would begin to howl too. Maybe I imagined it, but, just at that moment, I heard one wolf say to another: 'Shall we eat her, then?'

I didn't have the courage to wait for the reply. And since the beginning of the slope was some forty yards away, I broke into a trot, then a run. I ran, shaking the snow from the branches of the trees; and I was running and the wolves were running too, and I was panting and the wolves were panting too, and my breath was lost in the cold air, whilst the breath from the panting wolves, on the other hand, wasn't lost in the cold air, but on a part of my anatomy I prefer, out of politeness, not to mention. I felt more and more breath in that area, but the grove of trees was, at last, getting nearer and nearer.

Then, when I was sure I'd reached the slope, I felt something like a flame touch that unmentionable place and one of the wolves began to tug on the hairs at the end of my tail. I looked directly at it: it had pointed ears, reddish eyes, and a hairy mouth. Unfortunately for me, the hairs in its mouth were my hairs.

'We're lost, my friend!' I heard the voice say inside me.

'Don't you believe it! The wolf hasn't been born who could get the better of me!' I cried out wildly.

And with a strength born of desperation, I gave a huge leap and hurled myself headlong down the slope. It felt as if I were going to plunge into an abyss.

After flying through the air for a bit, I stumbled and finally rolled. If it hadn't been for the snow, I would surely have broken a bone or two, but the snow was soft and saved me.

'What about the wolves? Where are the wolves?' I asked myself. And while I was saying that, the same wolf who had tugged at the hairs on my tail, sank his teeth into that rather remote part of my anatomy. I gave a yelp of pain and, at the same time, dealt him a powerful kick that caught him full on. He ran off howling. He took with him his ears and his eyes, he took with him his mouth, but he didn't take with him the teeth in that mouth. They all fell out with that one blow. Soon afterwards, thanks in large part to The Pest, I was safe back in the barn at home.

Come to think of it, though, where are those winter snows now? Or rather, as I learned to say in French long after that incident with the wolves: *Où sont les neiges d'antan?* How many years have passed since they melted for ever? Because that's the truth of the matter, they melted, and our youth melted away with them. We were all young then: I was young, The Pest was young, the wolves were young, the other cows in my house were young, and even the century itself was young, it was only 1940 then; now the century is drawing to a close. Where has it all gone! Where are the snows of yesteryear? I realise now that then we were almost happy, and even The Pest and I got on better than it would seem. In fact, she hadn't become a complete Pest yet, and wasn't that irritating; true, she liked to get her own way, but she knew how to do so without giving orders. I was almost convinced that she really was my Guardian Angel. Lately, though, she just keeps on and on at me until she gets what she wants. On that night of thunder and lightning, for example, she didn't care how comfy I was in my bed, and she kept asking me that question over and over: 'Listen, my dear, has not the hour arrived? Is this not the appropriate, correct and convenient moment?'

When The Pest is in that mood, you might as well give in, because, otherwise, she simply won't shut up.

'What hour? It can't be time to get up yet! If it is, please just leave me in peace until day has dawned.'

'It isn't time to get up, my dear, but time to keep a promise that you made a long time ago. Do you remember what you said to me that night with the wolves?'

'I've no idea.'

'You've grown old and lazy, but despite that, I can't believe that you really don't remember. Because who can best remember her young days? Why, the cow who is getting on in years. She may not remember what happened the day before, but she can remember exactly what happened forty years ago. Anyway, I will tell you what you promised after escaping from the wolves. You said: "One day, I will write my memoirs and I will describe everything that happened tonight."'

'I don't believe you,' I said bluntly.

'Well, I find that hard to credit, because you said the same after that fiesta in the village, and again when you left home, and on many other occasions too. It was always the same old story: you would write your memoirs, you said.'

'I find that incredible!'

'Well, it's true. And now I come to think of it, when Green Glasses arrived at your house, you said the same again. According to you, that bitter episode would also appear in your memoirs.'

'Green Glasses! The ugliest creature I ever met!' I exclaimed, unable to contain myself.

'You see? You do remember, and very clearly! And do you know what I think? The century is moving on and so are you, and you can't depart this life just like any other cow. You must leave a testimony! Let the world know how great a cow can be! The hour has come, my dear, the moment has arrived!'

'Do you really think so?' I said in a resigned voice, for I knew I had no choice but to write my memoirs. If I didn't, as I said before, I would have to hear that same old song night after night.

'I'm positive, my dear. You must start writing.'

'In that case, I'll go and fetch pen and paper and I'll begin at first light.'

And that is what I did.

# Second Chapter

Why I do not return to Balanzategui, my birthplace. What Pauline Bernadette told me. The first major trauma — my birth.

Apparently, I had to be born and so I ended up being born in a wood in the Basque Country shortly after the end of the 1936 war. The wood was part of land belonging to a house called Balanzategui, and I became part of that household: there I lived in my first barn and had my first home, and there too I spent the early years of my life, the most important years. It's true that I didn't stay there very long, it's true that I've spent many years far from that house, but my spirit still misses that part of the world. And, who knows, perhaps my spirit flies there whenever I fall asleep. As a wise oriental once said:

THE BLACKBIRD FROM ISTANBUL
ALWAYS FLIES TOWARDS ISTANBUL.

I'm not a blackbird, a thrush or any kind of bird, for I'm rather too big and bulky for that, but it's no lie to say that my heart is not so very different from theirs. Indeed, my heart is the heart of a bird; if my heart had its way, it would have me spread my wings right now and fly away to the land of my childhood. I would arrive there, land all one thousand pounds of me as lightly as a snowflake, and then I would pour my feelings into this one cry: 'Long live Balanzategui!'

Of course, I don't have wings, and I can only move my body by planting my four feet on the ground, and even then it's quite an effort. And that is why I don't go back to Balanzategui, because of the effort involved and because of all the usual aches and pains that come with old age. If I felt strong enough, I would set off tomorrow. In fact, if I knew for certain how much longer I had to live, I would set off despite all my aches and pains. If, for example, they told me that I still had another two years of life, then I would try — slowly, unhurriedly, but I would certainly try. As the saying goes:

THE COW WHO WON'T TRY ONCE IS
EITHER A WEAKLING OR A DUNCE.

I don't believe I'm either of those things, and I would leave for Balanzategui today if I knew that I had those two years ahead of me. The trouble is, I don't know if I do or not. We cows are always unlucky; we were even unlucky on the day when time was shared out. I have heard that when the world began there was someone in charge of sharing out time, and that someone said to the snake: 'You will live for twelve years.'

And the snake said: 'Fine.'

To the dog: 'Fifteen years.'

And the dog said: 'Fine.'

To the donkey: 'Twenty-eight years.'

And the donkey said: 'Fine.'

To the man: 'Thirty-three years.'

And the man said: 'You must be joking. I can't accept that. I want to live longer.'

'All right, you will live for eighty-eight years,' the person who was sharing out time must have said, 'but of those eighty-eight years, you will spend thirty-three as a man, twenty-eight working like a donkey, fifteen leading a dog's life, and the last twelve you will spend crawling on your belly like a snake.'

Anyway, it seems that the matter of how long men would live was resolved and the sharing out of time continued. And so the ants, bees, butterflies, wrens, seagulls, kestrels, tortoises, camels, trout, lions, tigers and kangaroos all learned how much time they would have in the world. Then there came a moment when it was all over and the Sharer-out of Time was about to leave.

'And what about us? How many years will we

have?' someone was heard to say. Naturally, it was a cow. It seemed that everyone had forgotten about her.

They say that the Sharer-out of Time said wearily: 'How long? Hmm. Well, I don't know. A few years.'

'Thank you very much,' said the cow. And with that everyone said goodbye and went their separate ways.

That cow must have been a fool, a chump, a booby to respond to the Sharer-out of Time's 'A few' with a 'Thank you very much.' What did she mean 'Thank you very much'? That cow was nothing like me, of course.

I would have asked the Sharer-out of Time: 'What do you mean "a few"? Because, obviously, "a few" can mean almost anything. Three years could be a *few*, so could forty years or even two hundred years. It depends on how you look at it. So could you just clarify what you mean by "a few"?'

And the Sharer-out of Time would have clarified the point and told me exactly how many years I could expect. Let's say a hundred. That way, knowing how long you had in the world, you could then do your calculations.

'I came into the world around 1940, and the

century is now drawing to a close. That means that I've been in the world for fifty years. If I'm supposed to live for a hundred years, a hundred minus fifty is fifty. I still have fifty years left, so therefore it's worth my while to make my way slowly back to Balanzategui. Even if it took me ten years to get there, I would still have years and years to spend peacefully in the shade of the wood where I was born.'

But that cow at the beginning of the world was stupid, and she didn't ask how long our 'few years' would be. So there is no way I can know if it's worth my while making the journey back to Balanzategui, because though it's sad to have to die far from the place where you were born, it would be even sadder to have to say your final farewell in some unknown place en route. That's what Sister Pauline Bernadette says too; she's the little French nun who has looked after me for quite some time now:

'You won't be going anywhere, my dear, you're happy and comfortable here with us. Or don't you think so? Would you say we treated you badly here at the convent? What do you want? Do you want to leave here and end up with a broken back on some rough road somewhere?'

'In one way, you're right, Sister. Balanzategui

apart, this convent is my heart's true home, *ma vrai maison*,' I say to the little nun, struggling to speak her complicated language. And she really appreciates my words, about how the convent is my heart's true home and all that. She's so pleased, in fact, that before I know it, there's a big pile of grass in front of me, or, rather, grasses, because there's always a bit of everything in these piles, from fenugreek to clover to alfalfa.

'Careful, Sister!' I usually say, because it's good manners to protest a bit. 'You've given me far too much grass here. If this goes on, I won't be a cow, I'll be a hippopotamus. Since I came to the convent, I've gained forty pounds a year.

'Oh, but you were so thin that day when we first met, all those years ago!' the little nun says with a sigh. 'But you won't go hungry as long as I'm alive, my dear Mo, I'd scour the Pyrenees for grass if I had to!'

'You'd better not, Sister; the other cows have to eat too, you know,' I say, speaking in my own language now. Sister Pauline Bernadette may be small, but she's very strong and very good at physical work; she's a tireless scyther of grass. And given how fond she is of me, who knows, she might well strip the slopes of the Pyrenees bare.

Anyway, the reasons I dream about Balanzategui are not material ones, but spiritual ones. The convent and the little nun are fine, so are the alfalfa, the clover and the fenugreek, but in the words of the old song:

I LEFT MY HEART IN BALANZATEGUI...

Ah, my beloved Balanzategui! You're never far from my thoughts. I'm sure that many people, reading these words, will think, quite wrongly, that I'm lying, that I'm exaggerating like a mere beast. But you, dear childhood home, know the truth; for every time I shout out 'Long live, Balanzategui' there are a hundred more when I keep silent. And that's despite everything, despite all the setbacks and misfortunes we had to put up with during those years after the war. Just take my birth, for example. Do you remember, dear house, the dreadful time I had just after I was born and the dangers I encountered? I remember it all too well.

Suddenly, I knew that I had been born. I don't remember exactly what I felt, perhaps a breath of cold air or the tickle of the wind, but whatever it was, it seemed most unusual to me and probably had to do with my having come into the world. That, in fact, was the only thing I was sure about at that moment, because, knowing nothing, I didn't even know what kind of animal I was. I tried my best to look at myself and find out, but my eyes wouldn't obey me. It was as if I were blind, as if I were dazzled by a brilliant white sheet someone was holding up in front of me. Faced by that uncertainty, I had no option but to resort to my imagination, and that's what I did, possibly to excess.

'I wonder what I am,' I asked myself. 'There's no real way of finding out for sure,' I replied. 'But at least I'm not just any old animal. If I was, I wouldn't have come into the world on such a soft, pleasant piece of ground.'

To confirm my impression, I took a few steps up and down and felt the ground beneath me. And there it was, so soft, so pleasant.

'What can this soft stuff be?' I asked myself. 'One of two things — either a carpet in a palace or a carefully kept lawn in a garden,' I replied.

Since walking tired me, I lay down again. My body — in that first moment I weighed about eighty pounds — immediately felt comfortable, and the idea of the carpet began to gain credibility.

'It's like a Persian carpet,' I said to myself. 'That means that I'm some palace animal. It does seem rather a small palace, it's true, with no trees or fountains, but it's a palace nonetheless.'

By then, the sheet I could see before me was no longer quite as white; there were dark splodges on the upper part. They looked like trees, or, rather, the tops of several trees. At the same time — for it seems that my hearing was becoming sharper too — I heard the sound of water and the singing of birds.

'So it's not such a small palace,' I thought, giggling. 'It's got trees and fountains. I wonder what I am. One of those really elegant horses that gets brushed and combed every day? If not, what am I? One of those cats with long, soft fur that you usually find in palaces? Whatever I am, it's not bad, not bad at all.'

I don't know how much time passed — an hour perhaps, an hour and a half. Meanwhile, as the sheet before my eyes gradually dissolved, the splodges began to take shape. In the end, the sheet disappeared completely, and everything that had lain behind it was revealed. The trees stood out clearly and became whole trees with roots, trunk and branches. And on the branches there were leaves — dark green and light green. And on the leaves there were insects and larvae; and there were birds — especially ones with a red head — that arrived to eat those insects and larvae. Farther off, the wood

45

suddenly ended and beyond it was a meadow, a big meadow bordered by a stream. By the stream was a mill and behind the mill the woods began again.

'My dear,' I heard a voice say, and that was the first time I heard my Guardian Angel, The Pest, or whatever her name is, 'you have been born in the Basque Country, or to be more precise, more exact, in the wood above the house called Balanzategui. Beginning with the mill, this valley comprises all the houses and woods around it and this valley will be your territory.'

'But what am I?' I asked. That was my greatest concern, for I still did not dare to look at myself. 'That house you mentioned, Balanzategui, is it a palace?' I added. I thought it probably wasn't, because what I had beneath my feet was not a carpet, but moss.

The Pest had fallen silent, however, and I waited in vain for a reply. My heart was heavy — what kind of animal was I? But why drag things out, I just had to turn my head to find out. I turned my head, I saw what I saw, I saw the tail, the legs, the back and all the rest, and a heartrending cry emerged from within: 'I'm a cow!'

Overwhelmed by disappointment, stumbling, falling flat on my face and staggering to my feet again, I started to run, in order to get away from the wretched place that had witnessed the destruction of my first illusion. I left that meadow and, after crossing the meadow in front of the mill, I plunged into the wood on the other side of the valley. A moment before I did so, I heard the voice of The Pest again: 'My dear, before hiding yourself in the woods, take a look at your house. There's Balanzategui over there!'

The house was lower down in the valley, about a hundred yards from the old mill. It was a two-storey house, painted white with a red roof; it was quite a nice house, but it was no palace. Not that it mattered, of course. I was hardly palace-material; I wasn't a fine horse or an Angora cat, I was a cow, just a cow, a big, ugly, horrible animal, a disreputable dimwit. It really was most unfortunate.

'Life has played a very dirty trick on me!' I thought, bellowing and searching my memory for some swear word.

Since I had only just been born, however, I couldn't find any suitable word. I'd have no problem now, of course. I'd come out with a word that would knock Pauline Bernadette for six, not that I would, though, because she's the last person I'd want to shock, because almost anything shocks her. Once, for example, a boy who had come to the

47

convent threw a stone at me, and I got angry and I said: 'Go away, you pile of poo!'

And just at that moment, by some weird coincidence, the boy tripped and fell headlong into a pile of manure. He was covered, the poor thing. Pauline Bernadette, who had seen it all, opened her eyes wide in amazement.

'Sometimes you frighten me, my dear!' she exclaimed. 'You've got the devil inside you. We'll have to kneel down together again and see if we can rid you of that devil.'

'It wasn't the devil, Sister, it was just fate or chance. The boy just fell of his own accord, not because I wished it on him. I don't think we need to kneel down.'

Because of that business about ridding me of the devil, Pauline Bernadette is always trying to get me to kneel down, and sometimes there we are, the two of us, in the convent garden, bruising our knees and making complete fools of ourselves. But what can I do? As I said before, no one can beat the little nun when it comes to scything grass, and she brings me the most delicious grasses to eat, so I have to humour her.

But that's enough about Pauline Bernadette; let's get back to what happened on the day I was born. As I told you, I plunged into the wood feeling furious and disillusioned, and I began to go deeper and deeper in. I didn't want to know about Balanzategui, I never wanted to see it again. And, who knows, if I'd been strong enough, perhaps that's precisely what would have happened and I would have gone so far off that I would have lost my home for ever. I was still very weak, though, and I didn't even get beyond the valley. From time to time, I would stop, look at myself, then lift my head up and bellow mournfully: 'I'm a cow!'

I spent two days wandering about in that desperate state. On the third day, after having slept a few hours, I felt a bit calmer. The Pest took advantage of that moment to speak to me for the third time: 'My dear, what is all the fuss about? What is so awful about being a cow? It's wonderful to be a cow!'

'I don't care,' I moaned. 'I wanted to be a horse or a cat, not a cow. I wanted to live in a palace too, and look where I've ended up!'

The Guardian Angel, that is, The Pest, chortled. I think that was the first and last time that I heard her laugh.

'How little you know of life, my dear. What do you think palaces are like? Did you know that some of the best palaces in the world lacked certain vital necessities? Do you know, for example, what Versailles lacked?'

'What? A kitchen?'

'No, not a kitchen.'

'A stable?'

'No, not a stable.'

'Bedrooms?'

'No, not bedrooms.'

'An attic?'

'No, not an attic.'

'A junk room.'

'No, not a junk room.'

'So it must be...'

'Exactly, my dear, *that* is what it lacked. Ponder then the nature of palaces. They are pure appearance, my dear. Aside from that, they bring nothing but embarrassing dilemmas, awkward situations, fruitless searches. In Balanzategui, on the other hand, there is no such problem. The meadows, the wood, the hill, the barn itself — everything is allowed, everything is free, ready to satisfy you and your needs.'

I was so amazed at what I had just learned about palaces, that, for a moment, I forgot about the problem of my bovine nature, my shame at being a cow. The Pest roused me from my thoughts: 'As for that other idea of yours, that you would rather be a cat, for example, well, what can I say, my dear? I wouldn't want to cast aspersions on the way cats live, but it seems to me they have an awful time, and they don't get on at all well with each other, especially in the months of February and August. Just wait till then, my dear, and you'll hear their cries and screams of distress! Heartrending, truly heartrending! I don't know what it is, but something obviously happens to them then. And as you'll know, they spend a great deal of time walking about on rooftops, and that really can't be considered a serious occupation. As I say, I'm not one to speak ill of cats, but, given the choice, I would prefer to be a cow.'

'What about a horse, then? It must be wonderful to be a horse, don't you think?' I said.

'I don't deny that the horse does have its advantages. It's a large animal, sometimes even larger than a cow. And it can run very fast. The reality, though, is quite different: the horse doesn't know what it is to have a good night's sleep. It's too restless, too nervous. To my way of thinking, that is a major disadvantage, because such a large part of our lives is spent sleeping; so sleeping badly is equivalent to living badly. If you have a bad night, a bad day is sure to follow. So you see, my dear, although the horse certainly cuts a fine figure in this world, if I had to choose, I would prefer to be a cow. The cow sleeps peacefully, she always has a good rest, as you yourself have just discovered. See how calm you feel after a few hours' sleep.'

I remained thoughtful and, although the question of my bovine nature was still not fully resolved — that would come later — for the time being, I resigned myself to accepting it. I was only a young thing and I lacked the resources to argue with The Pest. Yes, I would have to put up with it. If I had to be a cow, then so be it.

'But I won't be just an ordinary cow!' I cried.

'Well said, my dear. And now off you go to Balanzategui. It would be best to get home before it's dark,' The Pest said, and I took her advice and began heading down into the valley. I would go to the old mill and from there to my house.

That was not quite what happened, however, for Green Glasses, the most evil person I have ever met, stood in my way.

# THIRD CHAPTER

GREEN GLASSES AND HIS TWO MINIONS. THE STORIES
ABOUT THE TOWER OF BABEL. LA VACHE QUI RIT SAVES
MY LIFE AND THEN TELLS ME ABOUT THE WAR THAT HAS
JUST ENDED.

I don't know how many things a person can see at any one time, whether it's ten, fifteen or forty-five, but when I came down from the wood to the old mill, I saw an enormous number of things. I saw the moon in the clear evening sky, and, in the distance, a big mountain, which, at that hour, lay half in darkness; and in front of that mountain, another smaller one; and in front of that smaller mountain, an even smaller one; and in front of that even smaller mountain, a long line of very gentle hills. But that isn't all I saw: as well as the moon, the sky and all those mountains, I saw the valley where I was born, with its wood, its meadows and its houses; one house on the left bank of the stream, another on the right bank, and then, a little closer, Balanzategui, and even closer, right before me, the old mill. And that still wasn't all I saw: as well as moon, sky, mountains, valley, woods, meadows, houses and mill, my eyes also saw four figures, not far along the very path on which I was standing: the first was a very elegant sorrel horse; the second was a young man with abnormally large teeth, possibly a builder, who was working on the roof of the mill; the third was the first man's equally large-toothed twin, who was also on the roof; the fourth was Green Glasses.

Green Glasses was a very pale man of about sixty. He had extremely white skin, or, to be more precise, his skin was as transparent as cigarette paper, so transparent that you could see the fine veins on his face and neck; his glasses seemed to be part of that extreme paleness and looked as if they were made out of bottle-green glass. When I saw him on that first occasion and whenever I met him afterwards, his eyes were always hidden behind his glasses.

I don't know how many things a person can see at any one time, I don't know how many things I saw when I came down the path out of the woods and stopped near the mill; what I do know is that I instantly forgot all of them, and every scrap of my attention, my curiosity, became fixed on those green glasses. I could see nothing else, only the green glass, and not even the shouts of the large-toothed brothers could make me look at them instead.

Suddenly, Green Glasses' lips curled into a sneer.

'Karral! Karral! Karral!' he said.

'What?' said the two toothy brothers on the roof.

'Karral! Karral! Karral!' repeated Green Glasses in a still harsher voice.

I couldn't understand a word. He was obviously speaking, but I had no idea what he was saying. He pronounced the words in a very strange way. Surprised, I asked myself: 'What *is* going on here?' But I couldn't answer that question. I was still a child, a new arrival who didn't even know that different languages and countries existed in the world, and that this was what was happening there; the man in the green glasses was a foreigner who spoke my language very badly. Or as Pauline Bernardette would have said:

'It's like the Tower of Babel all over again.'

Pauline Bernadette loves to mention the Tower of Babel whenever she can, well, she did until she told *me* the story and some quibble of mine very nearly ruined it for her.

'Once upon a time, many many years ago,' Pauline Bernadette began, 'mankind decided to build an incredibly tall tower that would reach up to the sky, because men wanted to be the equal of

Our Lord God. And they set to work with their picks and shovels and hoes, and everything was going swimmingly, with the tower growing taller and taller, until God split their single language into many languages. Suddenly, they could no longer understand each other, and since they couldn't make themselves understood, fights broke out and there was discord everywhere, and in the end, they had to abandon the work and the tower and everything and leave it just as it was, and everyone, each group with its new language, set off into the world, each to their own corner and their own country.'

'That's a lovely story, Sister. It's just a shame that it's a lie,' I said.

'A lie?' said the little nun, horrified. 'No. How can you say that, Mo?'

'Because it is a lie,' I answered coolly. 'How am I supposed to believe that they stopped building the tower simply because God created all those languages? To build something like that, you don't need to speak, you need to work. If God wanted to stop them building the Tower of Babel, why didn't he take away their picks and hoes and shovels? That's what I would have done if I'd been there, I'd have taken away their picks and hoes and shovels, and that would have been the end of it, farewell walls, farewell stairs, farewell everything.'

Pauline Bernardette stared at me wide-eyed when she heard this, and I was afraid she might get angry with me and make me kneel down. Instead, she started pacing back and forth in the convent garden, her eyes still wide, and she did this for at least half an hour. Then she said: 'When I lived in my village, in Altzürükü, our neighbour Pierre wanted to build a wall right next to our vegetable patch. But my father, who refused to accept such an absurd idea, went out one night and stole Pierre's hoe and pick and shovel and buried them. Then Pierre went and bought another hoe and pick and shovel. And my equally stubborn father buried them again. And so it went on. Finally, Pierre gave up and the wall was never built. Just as happened with the Tower of Babel. So I don't know quite what to think now about the story in the Bible.'

The little nun was still absorbed in her thoughts, and her wide, wide eyes frightened me. She was consumed by doubt, her religious faith all atremble like a building about to crumble to the ground. Naturally, I didn't want that to happen. If Pauline Bernadette left the convent, where would I get my fenugreek or my alfalfa?

'Yes, when you think about it,' I said, 'what

happened in Babel and what happened in Altzürükü with Pierre is almost the same, because when God created all the different languages and gave each group his own, what would have happened? Well, one man would say to the other "pass me the shovel", and the other man would pass him the hoe. Or vice versa. Or a third man would say "bring me a bucket of water for the mortar" and they'd bring him a couple of picks. And, of course, you can't possibly work in those conditions. So you see, the story of the Tower of Babel is quite right, much more so than I thought to begin with.'

Pauline Bernadette immediately recovered, and her eyes became their usual happy, carefree selves.

'It's true, Mo! Oh, that's such a weight off my mind. How wonderful. I do so appreciate your help, Mo.'

And with those words, she took up her scythe and walked over to a hillside near the convent to cut some lush grass for me to eat.

Anyway, as I said before, Pauline Bernadette's stories belong to a later period, not to the day when I met Green Glasses. At the time, I knew nothing about different languages and accents. And in a way, on that day at the windmill, this was fortunate, because I was so taken aback by how Green Glasses spoke, that my eyes detached themselves from the green of his glasses and fixed instead on the two toothy brothers, who were coming running towards me.

'Catch her! Catch her!' one brother was calling to the other.

'Come here, little one, we're going to have a real feast at your expense!' the other brother was saying, showing all his teeth.

I had a sudden flash of insight, like a lightning bolt: I understood that death existed and that it could take the form of a knife or a mallet. I could almost feel the knife in my heart and the mallet on my head. Yes, those two toothy brothers wanted to kill me. A shiver ran down my spine.

'Karral! Karral!' I heard a voice say. Green Glasses was laughing at me for being afraid.

His scorn angered me, and I went stumbling back up the path. If I could only get into the woods, I would be safe. I could feel the two brothers at my heels, cursing and huffing and puffing.

'You won't escape!' one of them yelled. He was closer than I thought.

The brothers were good, fast runners, and it soon became clear to me that they would catch me in the end. However, just when I was beginning to despair, a miracle occurred, the sort of miracle Pauline Bernadette is so fond of: a saviour appeared, or, rather, a saviouress, because she took the form of a black cow, who later, and for a very long time, I would know as *La Vache qui Rit* or The Laughing Cow. There she was, at the edge of the woods, giving the two brothers pursuing me a very hard stare.

'Watch out!' shouted one of the toothy ones. 'There's that really dangerous cow!'

They turned and were about to run back to the mill, but in vain, because *La Vache qui Rit* was too quick for them. *La Vache qui Rit*, that 'really dangerous cow', rushed at them before they had time to take refuge in the mill. One of the brothers ended up sprawled on the ground and the other one sought safety in the stream.

'Karral!' shouted Green Glasses. His mouth was all twisted and he was brandishing a stick as he heaped insults on the twins. That was when I first noticed his stick: it was covered in leather and had a sharp spike on the tip.

'Karral!' he shouted again, this time addressing his horse, which, having, up until then, been sunk in his own little world, had started neighing loudly. The Pest was right: splendid and elegant he might be, but the horse was too highly strung, too easily scared.

'There's no doubt about it, my friend,' said The Pest, hearing my thoughts. 'As I said before, horses don't sleep well at night and so, at any time of the day, they can be overcome by the need for a nap. That's what happened to this horse; he dropped asleep and was startled awake by the ruckus going on around him.'

'Karral! Karral!'

Green Glasses was beside himself with rage and made as if to hit the horse with his stick.

I realised that everyone had forgotten about me, and so decided to follow the example of *La Vache qui Rit*. On the one hand, seeing the nervous state the horse was in, I had begun to feel rather proud to be a cow, and on the other, I wasn't in the least afraid, you bet I wasn't, and I wanted to repay the toothy twins for frightening me like that.

Picking up speed as I ran down the hill, I went straight for the brother who, at that very moment, was clambering out of the stream.

'You don't know that black cow. She's very dangerous, completely mad,' he was saying to Green Glasses, pointing at *La Vache qui Rit*, who was standing by one of the doors to the mill.

He had barely finished speaking when I butted him hard. I heard a noise then, like the noise you make when you step on a dry twig in the wood.

'Could I have broken a horn?' I thought. But, no, the toothy twin was moaning and screaming, clutching one wrist.

'She's broken my wrist!'

'Karral!' screamed Green Glasses. He stuck his stick in the ground and went over to the horse. Hanging from the saddle was a holster with a rifle in it.

'Quick, run. Follow me!' shouted *La Vache qui Rit*.

I came all over goose pimples, and raced after her towards the Balanzategui woods. By the time Green Glasses had taken aim at us, we were safe and not far from the place where I'd been born not long before.

A lot of time has passed since then, but I still ask myself this question: why those goose pimples when *La Vache qui Rit* called to me to follow her? The tension of the moment? The danger? Or because someone, for the first time, was treating me like a friend? I don't know, but whatever the reason, that was a big day for me.

*La Vache qui Rit* was ugly and rather ill-proportioned, for she was much smaller than most cows, with a short neck and legs, but she had a very strong chest, a large head and powerful shoulders. As I said before, she was the same colour as me: black.

'How many bones have you broken so far?' she asked after kneeling down on the mossy floor of the wood.

'I'm sorry?'

I had to ask her to repeat the question because The Pest had prevented me from hearing what she said.

'My dear, the best thing you can do is to live according to a timetable,' The Pest had said. 'It's dark and time to go home. Leave the midnight hour for the owl, the bat and other nocturnal animals, and go home and rest. If you have a bad night, a bad day is sure to follow.'

Nevertheless, and despite my extreme youth, I was determined not to listen to The Pest's advice. I preferred to stay with *La Vache qui Rit*. After all, I owed her my life. And with that thought still in my head, I knelt down beside her.

'Good for you. It's dark now, but you're still not in a hurry to go home and sleep,' said *La Vache qui Rit*. 'You're clearly no fool. Most of the cows in

Balanzategui are, and all they think about is eating and sleeping. Absurd creatures. You seem quite different, and just as well, because there's nothing in this world more stupid than a stupid cow.'

'I'm sure you're right,' I said humbly.

'Anyway, don't you worry. Even if we don't go back for a couple of hours, the doors to the barn at Balanzategui will still be open. In this house, we cows do as we wish, it's like a paradise for cows. No discipline, no work, and on top of that, occasional banquets.'

'Banquets?'

'Yes, banquets. Sometimes it's for the red cows and sometimes for the black ones like us, although more often than not, it's for us. And the banquets are quite something. You'll see.'

'My dear,' I heard the Pest say, 'promise me one thing, that you'll return to the barn once you've said goodbye to this friend of yours. Say goodbye nicely and go back home and have a peaceful night's sleep. Besides, you need to get to know the other cows at Balanzategui.'

I again ignored The Pest. I was determined to continue talking to *La Vache qui Rit*. There were so many things I wanted to know, that the questions were piling up. What were these banquets? Who were Green Glasses and his two minions? And what were they doing in the mill? I ran out of breath. As the saying goes:

A CURIOUS COW ALWAYS WANTS TO KNOW WHY, WHERE AND HOW.

But *La Vache qui Rit* was in no hurry and, ignoring my questions, she began examining me from head to hoof. Her eyes were very bright.

'So, tell me, was that the first bone you've ever broken?' she asked after a pause. She seemed not to notice that I had not long entered this world.

'Well, yes,' I said, feeling slightly intimidated.

'You must break more, many more. A cow who goes through life without breaking twenty or thirty bones is a stupid cow. Very stupid!'

'Listen, my dear,' said The Pest, interrupting. 'It's fine to make friends, but don't get too carried away with the first one you meet. Other friends await you in Balanzategui, and you should introduce yourself to them.'

In my present situation, I found The Pest's intervention rather troubling. I shifted slightly and changed my position.

'What's wrong? Is it your inner voice speaking to you?' said *La Vache qui Rit* casually. It would seem that the inner voice was one of our characteristics, something all cows carry within them. I nodded. Yes, that was why I felt so troubled.

'It bothers me too,' *La Vache qui Rit* went on, looking up at the dark night and speaking in a slow, pensive voice. 'There's something not quite right about mine though. My inner voice doesn't sound like the voice of a cow at all. It's always talking about the same things, about fighting and battling and attacking. "Go on, lay into him, go for it," that's the kind of thing I hear, or else it tells me to leave Balanzategui and the barn: "Leave now. Go into the woods, that's where your true home is." I really don't understand it. Anyone would think I'd been given the voice of a wild boar, not a cow.'

Her eyes were shining more brightly than ever, and her gaze was fixed on some point between the woods and the moon. I didn't say a thing. On the one hand, it didn't seem possible that she could have been given the wrong voice, on the other, there *was* something wild and surly about *La Vache qui Rit*. The toothy twins at the mill had said as much: she wasn't a normal cow, she was a dangerous cow.

'And what about *your* inner voice?' she asked, suddenly emerging from her thoughts.

'She speaks well, although rather slowly. The only thing I know for sure is that she's always very much in favour of being a cow. She prefers that to anything else.'

'Well, at least that's something,' said *La Vache qui Rit* somewhat vaguely, her mind elsewhere.

'Nasty people, those men at the mill,' she then said, revealing her current preoccupation. 'Those twins with the big teeth are a very nasty pair, but the one with the glasses is even worse. Yes, the old man is so dangerous that even my inner voice, which is normally itching for a fight, warns me to leave him well alone. The twins are no problem, they're just stupid peasants, local men, but you need to watch the old man. He's obviously a foreigner, and loves knives and swords and so on. You've seen the big stick he carries.'

I looked over at the mill. The walls were white in the moonlight.

'What are they doing in that mill?' I asked *La Vache qui Rit*.

'That's where the twins live, but the real boss now is the old man. He started coming to the mill about a month ago and he ordered them to do some work on the place. As you saw, they were both labouring away.'

'They seemed to be repairing the roof,' I said, wanting to help the conversation along.

'No, they're not retiling it, they're putting in a big window. And that's what I don't understand. Why put a window in the roof? To look at the stars? I'd love to know.'

'Listen, my child,' I heard my inner voice say. 'It seems to me that they're putting in that window so that they can keep watch on something. Not on the stars, though, because that Green Glasses fellow might be many things, but he's certainly no astronomer. Just think a little. What would you be able to see from that window when they've finished?'

'The place we are now, Balanzategui!' I thought, then immediately communicated my thought to *La Vache qui Rit*.

'I think that window could be used to keep an eye on Balanzategui. There'll be someone on permanent watch up there.'

*La Vache qui Rit* nodded approvingly.

'Good! I'm glad you said that. I was testing you out to see if you had any brains or not, and you've certainly proved that you have! I'm glad, really glad, to find that you're not a stupid cow, because there's nothing in this world more stupid than a stupid cow.'

I gave a sigh of relief, pleased to have impressed

*La Vache qui Rit*. Wordlessly — that is, purely in my thoughts — I thanked The Pest for her help.

'That's exactly right. Knives wants to keep watch on our house,' *La Vache qui Rit* said. Knives was her name for Green Glasses. 'Why? I don't know. That's why I spend most of my time at the top of the hill, watching the mill and listening to what they're saying. Not that Knives is a blabbermouth, and he tells the toothy twins very little. And, worse, I find it really hard to understand him.'

'I don't find it hard, I find it impossible. But do you really not know what he's up to?'

*La Vache qui Rit* looked at me very seriously. No, she wasn't testing me out this time.

'I don't know anything for certain, but I've drawn my own conclusions.'

'Which are?' I asked with the innocence of a cow newly arrived in the world.

*La Vache qui Rit* looked at me even more seriously with those bright eyes of hers.

'Have you heard anything about the war?' she said after a pause.

'No, I haven't.'

'That's only natural in one so young, but I'm a bit older and I've seen a few things in this world, and the war was one of them. Look at our valley, look at the sky above, those hills and woods...'

*La Vache qui Rit* broke off and fell silent. For my part, I did as I was told and stared up at the moon. In the early dark, there was not a sound in the valley, or only those carried to us now and then on the south wind.

'Yes, now everything's quiet and peaceful,' *La Vache qui Rit* went on. 'But you should have seen this valley a year ago or perhaps less. Rifle fire at all hours of the day and night. And gun fire too sometimes. And then there were the planes, machine-gunning everything and killing every living creature. One of those planes was shot down just near here, at the other end of the valley. A very pretty plane, small and silvery.'

'Where?' I said, suddenly excited. 'I'd love to see it.' I'd never seen a plane.

'Ah, then you would know what I know, my friend,' said *La Vache qui Rit* somewhat cuttingly. 'The plane is my secret, and I'm the only one who knows where it is. I might show you one day, though, we'll see.'

*La Vache qui Rit* gave me a long look. She was still in two minds as to whether I was a stupid cow or not. She wouldn't want to show the fallen plane to a stupid cow.

'I'll find it even if you don't show it to me,' I retorted, trying to be as cutting as she had been. 'But let's get back to the matter of the war and what's happening at the mill.'

*La Vache qui Rit* looked up. She liked my response.

'Well, as I say, until very recently, there was a war going on here,' she began, in a friendlier tone of voice this time. 'Between soldiers on the two sides. And many of them died. In fact, three of them died right here in this wood.'

'Three men?'

'Yes, three men. They were killed not far from here. Genoveva's husband was one of them.'

I was aflame with curiosity and in such a hurry to know what had happened that I asked breathlessly:

'Genoveva's husband? But who's Genoveva?'

'The owner of Balanzategui, of course! Who else?' cried *La Vache qui Rit* angrily. I thought she might lose patience with me, but if she was a cow with character, so was I.

'How am I supposed to know that, when I've never set foot in the barn at Balanzategui! I've been out and about on the hills,' I said firmly.

'Yes, of course, of course,' agreed *La Vache qui Rit* in a conciliatory tone. 'Anyway, like I say, Genoveva is the name of the owner of Balanzategui.'

I sensed that her respect for me was growing. That was clearly the way to speak to *La Vache qui Rit*.

'They shot her husband when the war was just about to end. Her husband and two other men. Do you want to see their graves?'

'Oh, yes!' I exclaimed.

We took the path that led directly to the house, which was visible at that hour thanks to its white walls and the moonlight, then, just before we reached the house, we veered off slightly into the woods and came to a garden planted with trees. However full of flowers, though, that place wasn't a garden, but a cemetery, as shown by the three wooden crosses that rose up above the flowers.

'Genoveva's husband and his two friends. They were shot right here,' said *La Vache qui Rit*, kneeling down at the edge of the cemetery. In the moonlight, the colours were all confused: the red flowers looked black, and the white ones blue. The moss covered the ground like a carpet.

'When did the war end exactly?' I asked softly, not daring to kneel down. Since being pursued by the twins at the mill, I knew what a grim thing death was, and the three crosses in the cemetery aroused in me a feeling akin to fear. But *La Vache qui Rit* was used to the place, and it didn't trouble her. She asked me to kneel by her side.

'That's what I ask myself,' she said once I'd joined her. She was speaking to me openly now, as if to an equal. 'I wonder if the war really has ended. They say it ended a year ago, and that seems mostly to be true, because now you don't hear rifle or gun fire. On the other hand, I'm not so sure. I have a feeling the war is still going on. At least it is here in Balanzategui. And that's why Knives and the others are watching the house.'

'Who?' I asked, having forgotten the name *La Vache qui Rit* gave to Green Glasses.

'The men at the mill,' she answered, still deep in thought. Then she sighed and said something that made me sit up and take notice. 'Yes, it's true. Some very strange things go on in this house, very strange.'

She grew silent and thoughtful again, as if she had completely forgotten about me. For my part, I would have liked to ask more questions: what did she mean and what were those 'strange things', but I didn't dare open my mouth. It seemed rude to ask so many questions, childish. As the saying goes:

MORE QUESTIONS, FEWER ANSWERS.

75

Since *La Vache qui Rit* seemed disinclined to leave her meditations, I said nothing and merely gazed at the crosses in that small cemetery. Genoveva's husband. A friend of his. And another friend too. Three soldiers shot dead. Had the war ended in Balanzategui? Did the strange things *La Vache qui Rit* had mentioned have something to do with those deaths? Yes, they probably did.

'My dear,' I heard a voice say then. It was The Pest speaking to me from inside. 'I've been thinking too, and this is what I thought: at one point, this rather surly cow, who calls herself *La Vache qui Rit*, said something I found very odd: she said that Balanzategui was a paradise for cows and that in this house, which, by the way, you still don't know, despite me advising you to go there, well, she said that in this house, the cows have no work to do, there's no discipline, and that sometimes there are banquets... and when you think about it, isn't that all rather odd?'

The Pest was probably right. I remembered *La Vache qui Rit* using the words 'paradise' and 'banquets', and that *was* rather odd. I turned to *La Vache qui Rit* and was about to ask her a question, one question, a very pertinent one this time.

However, I didn't have time to do so. The

small cemetery was suddenly filled by a strange, spinechilling noise that made me ask a different question: 'What kind of animal makes a noise like that?'

In my imagination, as if in a dream, I could see that creature: it was a huge bird with blue feathers and flapped its wings rather like an eagle.

'What are you talking about?' asked *La Vache qui Rit*, seeing me staring up at the sky. 'It's not a bird, it's one of Genoveva's records, violin music, if you must know. Genoveva often listens to records, not every night, but now and then. Let's go into the barn, which is immediately underneath her living room. You can hear the music better there than anywhere.'

I liked the idea. I didn't know what a record was, but I found the sound it produced very moving. As the saying goes:

BEETHOVEN, CHOPIN AND
MENDELSSOHN BRING JOY TO COWS AND
EVERYONE.

'We'll talk more about the war later. We still have much to discuss,' *La Vache qui Rit* whispered to me just before we went into the barn.

Once inside, the violin music wrapped about me. I was finally in Balanzategui, my home. And when the cows gathered there greeted me, how are you, Mo, welcome, Mo, come on in, Mo, I felt like someone. It was no small thing being a cow.

# Fourth chapter

My easy life in Balanzategui and its ill effects.
Genoveva's personality. They lay on a banquet for
the black cows. What happened on the night
of the banquet.

With my arrival, there were twelve cows at Balanzategui, five red ones and seven black ones. As *La Vache qui Rit* had warned me, most were pretty stupid, the kind of cow who thinks only of eating and sleeping; there was, however, a more positive side, for they were all very friendly and affectionate, always ready to help. Both red and black cows were equally eager to spend time with me, to talk to me, go with me to the fields or drink water from the stream. And during all that time, my tender newly-arrived-in-the-world ears heard only kind words: 'Mo, do try this alfalfa; Mo, come and join me in the shade.' One day passed and then another, and everything remained the same; my life followed the easiest and most comfortable of paths.

Perhaps it was all too easy, I don't know. Or rather, I do know, it really *was* much too easy, and I ended up becoming a lazy, indolent cow, incapable of leaving the comforts of Balanzategui. From the barn to the fields opposite, and from the fields opposite to the barn, that was as far as I went. I lived glued to the walls of that house, like a fly to a jar of honey.

'And what about your mind?' someone might ask. 'What was going on in your mind?' Well, as you might expect, my mind wasn't much better than that of the most fly-brained fly, and quite incapable of thinking anything. For example, it didn't even realise how badly I was behaving towards *La Vache qui Rit* by not going anywhere near the mill and not helping her keep an eye on Green Glasses & Co. It's true that, everyday, I did think about going to see her, but night would come and there I was with my four feet still firmly planted in the sweet mud of Balanzategui. There were even times when I would recall the conversation we'd had by the little cemetery and I would order myself to go to her and find out more about the war; in the end, though, I always put off following my own orders. As the saying goes:

A FLY-BRAINED COW THINKS ONLY
OF NOW.

And that was precisely the case with me, and, as a consequence, I risked losing a friend. A true friend, I mean, because apart from *La Vache qui Rit*,

I had no friends at Balanzategui: I had companions, yes, but no friends.

And yet it wasn't only the stupid cows who were responsible for the honey-pot existence I led in Balanzategui. There was another reason to stay near the barn, and that reason was Genoveva, the owner of the house.

At the time, Genoveva would have been at least fifty, and she was a very serious person, a woman of few words. Looking back now and with what I've learned from life so far, my impression is that she was the very opposite of Pauline Bernadette, for while Genoveva was all strength and sobriety, Pauline was all lightness and joy and contradictions. It's as if that little nun has not just one heart, but ten, ten hearts scattered hither and yon, as small as the little bells cats wear round their neck; ten hearts that never agree and all of which have a different ring to them. This is why she gives answers like the one she gave me recently after a visit to her village:

'I've had such a lovely day, Mo!' she began contentedly, ringing a few very high-pitched bells. 'It's been so long since I saw my mother and my father. But it was so sad when I had to say goodbye, Mo, so sad!' she went on, ringing a grave and melancholy bell. 'And do you know? They've done away with

the bus to Altzürükü! They have no right! she concluded, really annoyed now and angrily jingling all
her remaining bells.

Genoveva, the owner of Balanzategui, didn't
have that same abundance of hearts, she had only
one, solid and deep; a heart that made a sound like
the bells we cows sometimes wear. That heart was
not easily moved, it wasn't set jangling by mere
nonsense; but when it was moved, when something
struck that heart hard, the sound it made was terrible
and sombre, capable even of bursting the very walls
of her chest. This was perhaps a consequence of
seeing her husband shot dead, yes, perhaps that
had cast a permanent shadow over her heart and
her character.

Genoveva organised life in Balanzategui almost
single-handedly. She did have a servant we used
to call Stoopback, an old man who ran errands for
her and did a few other jobs. Not that Stoopback
could be of much help because — as you might
guess from the nickname we gave him — he was in
a terrible state physically, and also because he only
spent the mornings in Balanzategui. At midday, he
would get on his bike and cycle off to the village for
his lunch, always slowly, very slowly, as if afraid
he might fall off. It seemed that Genoveva only kept

him on for a bit of company, and I'm quite right to say 'seemed' because, in the end, he would surprise us all. Stoopback was just one of the many strange things about that house. Another was that there were no dogs or chickens or pigs, which you would expect to find in most houses in the valley. Equally strange was the fact that no one, neither Genoveva nor Stoopback, knew how to handle a scythe, not necessarily as skilfully as Pauline Bernadette, but not even reasonably well. But I won't go on about the many strange things in Balanzategui now. I will talk about them when the time comes. As the saying goes:

IF YOU WANT TO KNOW HOW IT ALL TURNS OUT, OPEN THE BOOK AT THE END AND NOT AT THE START.

Genoveva was a strong-minded woman, who never showed her feelings, not even when she went to the little cemetery in the woods and knelt down by the three crosses, and so reserved was she in both word and gesture that any word or gesture from her took on enormous importance. We all felt the same: if she greeted you by name, you felt happy all day, if she gave you a pat on the back, then life was almost a celebration. And one day, that strong, reserved woman called me over to her side, saying:

'So you're the new black cow!'

Those words were enough for me to feel I was the happiest cow in the world and to kneel at her feet. When I think about it now, what can I say? That it really wasn't such a big deal, and that, at the time, I was clearly a fly-brained creature? But every age is different, and you have to accept that. Now I'm looked after by Pauline Bernadette, which is a piece of good fortune very few deserve, but I'm old now, and the kind of happiness that usually goes hand in hand with innocence is no longer within my grasp. Then, though, I lived among people whose lives were very difficult, when the aftermath of the war was all too evident, but I was young and rather frivolous, and living was easy.

However, happiness was not the only consequence of Genoveva's words. Her way of speaking to me gave me a certain prestige, and the other stupid cows began to treat me as if I were important. And so the honeypot that was Balanzategui seemed even sweeter, and I barely gave a thought to *La Vache qui Rit*. I only noticed her when she came into the barn to listen to one of Genoveva's records or for some other special reason. She always arrived at night, and went to her corner without saying a word to anyone. Once there, she would raise her head and give us all a long, withering look, meaning: 'There's nothing more stupid than a stupid cow!'

At first, I found it very hard to accept her behaviour, because, with my fly-sized brain, I couldn't understand it: I attributed it to her bad character, and thought she was a very bad friend. Of course, the exact opposite was true. I was the bad friend, the one who was snubbing her. As I said before, I never went to the mill and showed no inclination to continue our conversation about the war.

I slowly forgot about everything that had happened. Green Glasses and the toothy twins seemed to me like characters out of some ancient nightmare; the stories about the ending or non-ending of the war felt like stories as old as Stoopback himself; the plane that had crashed nearby or the crosses in the little cemetery seemed of no significance. And yet I didn't forget everything, if I had, that would have been the end of the friendship between *La Vache qui Rit* and me. Everything began to mend between us one autumn day when we cows were summoned to one of Balanzategui's famous banquets.

I was in the woods along with the other cows,

resting for a moment on the fallen leaves, when suddenly Genoveva and Stoopback appeared.

'Up you get, all of you!' cried Stoopback, poking us with a stick.

'Come on! Quickly!' said Genoveva, looking more serious than ever. Being cows, it took us a while to get up, but, finally, we rejoined the path and went back to the house. When we were all outside the barn, Stoopback began counting us, clapping us each on the back as he did so.

'Eleven!' he said. 'Who's missing?' he asked Genoveva.

'Who do you think? That ugly, arrogant cow!' muttered the red cow called Bidani, the same one who had told me about the Guardian Angel.

'Why do you say that? *La Vache qui Rit* isn't arrogant,' I exclaimed.

'Of course she is. Only an arrogant cow would call herself *La Vache qui Rit*. Her real name is Bighead! Why else does she always keep herself to herself? Because she's stupid and arrogant,' retorted Bidani.

She wasn't normally so disagreeable, but her impatience to find out which of the two groups was going to get the banquet — whether the red cows like her or the black ones — had sharpened her tongue.

For my part, I didn't do or say anything else. It wounded me to hear Bidani's words, but the idea that I should say something more in *La Vache qui Rit*'s defence didn't even cross my mind, my fly-brained mind. It was really shameful on my part, and the way I behaved then still weighs on me, because, of course, you should always defend the people you care about against everything, against wolves, against stupid cows, against slander, against the wretches who repay kindness with cruelty, against everyone. At the age I am now, I never fail anyone, and I defend my people, Pauline Bernadette for example, even when she doesn't want me to.

In fact, that reminds me of something that happened not long ago in the convent. On the day in question, Pauline Bernadette did something that is absolutely forbidden in an enclosed order of nuns: she opened the gates and let outsiders into our garden, in this case, six young people with rucksacks and walking boots, who turned up in the portico of the chapel asking permission to pitch their tent.

'Can we put up our tent in one of the areas inside, Sister? We would feel much safer in your garden than out in a field somewhere,' they said to Pauline Bernadette. The group consisted of three girls and three boys, and their spokesperson was a fair-haired lad.

The convent does indeed resemble a citadel, because it's huge, and contains just about everything, from the actual convent building itself to all that you might expect on a big farm: pastures, maize fields, chicken runs, barns for the normal cows and barns for the special cows like me, rows and rows of fruit trees, sheds for the machinery, kitchens where the nuns make chocolate and jam... so there was plenty of space, and the young people could have camped anywhere. The problem was — as I mentioned before — that the laws of an enclosed order forbid strangers from entering the convent. And that is precisely what Pauline Bernadette said to those young people.

'But, Sister,' the young spokesperson said, 'you can't leave us outside. There's nothing but open countryside and we're afraid, especially the girls. They're really afraid. Couldn't you let us in through a side door?'

Pauline Bernadette hesitated. Her head told her that she must obey the convent rules and that, besides, it wasn't exactly a dangerous area, indeed, her own village of Altzürükü was close by; but all her hearts, those ten hearts of hers like bells on a cat's collar, told her the opposite, and demanded that she give shelter to those people asking for her help.

'A nun should obey the convent rules, but *charité* comes before all else,' she told herself.

Shortly afterwards, a small door at the back of the convent was opened to allow the young walkers in.

'Please, stay here, but, I beg you, be very quiet, and tomorrow you must leave at first light. If my Mother Superior finds out what I've done, I'll pay for it. A month's penance at the very least,' she told them once she'd led them to a lovely meadow in the garden.

The young people nodded and began putting up their tent. I, for my part, had my doubts. I didn't like the way their spokesman laughed.

Nothing happened until night fell, because, as far as I was concerned, the occasional guffaws issuing from the tent were nothing. Then, when it was dark, the three boys and three girls came out and started fooling around. They went over to one of the rows of trees and started picking cherries, but they behaved like vandals, even breaking off one whole branch just to pick a handful of cherries. They were clearly slightly drunk.

'Didn't I tell you we'd be able to stuff ourselves with cherries,' shouted the fair-haired boy, revealing what his true intentions had been when he approached Pauline Bernadette. 'And isn't this the most amazing place?' he added boastfully.

'Ungrateful people who repay good with evil are the very worst kind,' I thought to myself. You'd have to be the lowest of the low to play such a dirty trick on someone like Pauline Bernadette.

During supper, they drank a lot and laughed even more, guffawing and shouting so loudly they could have been heard in Altzürükü. How long would it take for the Mother Superior to be woken by that racket? I felt more and more anxious and preoccupied, and found it hard to stay where I was in the barn.

When the guffaws and shouts had reached their peak, a shadowy figure armed with a stick strode across the garden. It was Pauline Bernadette. She was very angry and frightened too.

'How dare you! Get out of here, you philistines! Leave the convent at once!'

The group continued to make just as much noise as before, except that now they were staring at Pauline Bernadette.

'What a tiny little nun! Have you ever seen such

a tiny nun?' yelled the fair-haired boy. And the other boys and girls found this remark absolutely hilarious.

'Philistines!' said Pauline Bernadette, and, wielding her stick, she smashed a few of the beer bottles that had been left outside the tent.

While the others were mere idiots pure and simple, the fair-haired boy was a truly nasty piece of work. Sneering, he stood up in front of the tent and gave Pauline Bernadette a shove, before unleashing a whole string of foul language.

Pauline Bernadette's little bells fell suddenly silent. She was lost for words. And the fair-haired boy continued with his offensive jokes and cackling laughter, accompanied by his fellow idiots.

'The time has come to break another couple of bones, Mo,' I told myself. I couldn't allow them to treat Pauline Bernadette like that. I couldn't fail her as I had once failed *La Vache qui Rit*.

The fair-haired boy's insults and boasts stopped at once. When he saw me come out of the barn, he picked up one of the bottles Pauline Bernadette had smashed and tried to play the part of the big man in front of his friends. His legs were shaking though.

'Imbecile!' I thought. 'Who do you think you're fooling? Do you think I was born yesterday? Don't you realise that I know you're actually pooing your pants? You won't be threatening me with that bit of broken glass for long!'

I lowered my head and raised my horns as I put my one thousand pounds of flesh and bone into motion, and I broke his arm in two places. Then a lot of things happened, there were more screams and blows than had ever been heard in that garden, but why describe what anyone can so easily imagine?

'But Mo, why did you take vengeance into your own hands? That's very wrong!' Pauline Bernadette said when the young people had fled the garden. Despite her words, though, I knew that her little bells were jingling with joy.

You must always defend your friends, always. Against idiots, against your fellow cows, against whoever; you must always defend your friends. And yet, this isn't a truth we learn quickly. For example, I didn't know this during my first few months in Balanzategui, when I had the brain of a fly, which is why I didn't call Bidani to account for what she'd said about *La Vache qui Rit*, or Stoopback, who also insulted her for coming late to the banquet.

'Where's that ugly, big-headed cow?' Stoopback cried, once he'd finished counting those of us gathered in front of the barn.

'She'll be over at the old mill, where she always is. Maybe we can just leave her outside,' said Genoveva with her usual seriousness.

'But what if she joins the red cows? I know she wouldn't usually, but you never know. It's best if she comes into the barn too.'

'I'll whistle,' said Genoveva. She was a very good whistler, and that day she gave a long, loud whistle. She could whistle really musically too, and sometimes she would reproduce, note for note, the pieces she listened to on her records.

She didn't have to whistle again. *La Vache qui Rit* appeared down below in the stream, and with an energy that no one else in Balanzategui possessed, she trotted up the hill to the house in no time at all. She might be ugly and have a big head, but she was superior in strength to any other cow. She was, besides, brave and intelligent. Stoopback himself acknow-ledged this as soon as she joined the group, placing herself right by the barn door, as if eager to go in.

'In you go,' said Stoopback, opening the door. 'You're no fool, are you? You must have guessed that today's banquet is for you black cows!'

And, it was true, the banquet was for us. When one of the red cows, Bidani or whoever, tried to come into the barn, Stoopback would drive them away with a flick of his stick.

'You watch out, my dear, things are starting to happen here,' I heard my inner voice say. 'Remember what we talked about one day, about how strange I thought these banquets were,' she added.

I remembered then that we had once spoken about the bad people at the mill, about the war and the banquets...

All the excitement surrounding the banquet was doing me good. I was beginning to wake up, to emerge from the stupor into which the good life had plunged me, and my fly-sized brain was showing signs of being able to remember things. With that cheering thought, I started going into the barn with the other black cows.

'Don't be in such a hurry, my dear,' said The Pest. 'Why so rash and impetuous when it comes to entering the barn? Why don't you linger a while and enjoy the autumn breeze and, in passing, find out what the red cows are ordered to do? I think it's time to collect a little information. Otherwise, we'll never understand the strange things that go on in this house.'

I did as The Pest suggested, and, moving away from the barn door, I trotted off towards the red cows.

'Oh no you don't. In you go,' said Genoveva as soon as she saw what I was doing. She and Stoopback were herding the red cows towards a small circular area surrounded by a stone wall. That was very unusual too. Normally, they wouldn't let us in there, even when the grass was really long.

'Inside, I said! Into the barn with you!' shouted Genoveva. I delayed no longer and set off to join my fellow black cows. I had the information The Pest was asking for: I knew where they put the red cows while we were being given our banquet, and where they would put us on the day when the banquet was for the red cows.

'Why do they separate us into two groups whenever there's a banquet?' I wondered. I felt increasingly wide awake and very far from being a fly-brained creature.

Unfortunately, I couldn't talk to anyone about this. *La Vache qui Rit* didn't appear to want a reconciliation. She still wasn't speaking to me and, when she looked at us, her eyes expressed her usual belief: 'There's nothing in this world more stupid than a stupid cow!'

In that situation, it was impossible to attempt a conversation with her, and so I concentrated on the food in the trough.

When I look back now, with the experience life gives us, I wouldn't consider what they gave us that day in Balanzategui to be a banquet. After all, it was just fodder, a whitish stuff that arrived now and then by the sackload in a Chevrolet pickup truck. Of course, in those days, we cows had only tasted food from outside, and the fodder seemed a huge novelty, as huge a novelty, it must be said, as that Chevrolet pickup truck that ran on four wheels. For those were very different times. The only mechanical contraption seen in the valley until then had been the fallen airplane that *La Vache qui Rit* had mentioned.

As well as being a novelty, the fodder had a slightly spicy taste, a stronger flavour than the grass we ate every day, and we ate it with pleasure. After two or more hours of pure indulgence, we knelt down to digest our food. We stayed in the barn, you understand, because Genoveva and Stoopback waited until the following morning before opening the barn doors.

The day of my first banquet, I felt very well. Not just because of the food, but also because of the records Genoveva played in her living room. However, despite the peace that reigned in Balanzategui, The Pest was still worried. She couldn't understand the reason for that banquet.

'Listen, my dear. Why the fodder? With all the excellent, tasty, nutritious grass there is in Balanzategui, why bother having a pickup truck deliver this special food? Each sack must be quite expensive. To be honest, it seems a waste of money. Besides, it's not a healthy way to eat. Whenever possible, you should eat naturally, otherwise you might damage one of your stomachs. And, believe you me, any cow who damages one of her stomachs, damages a part of her life. Natural is best, my dear. Whenever possible, eat naturally. I really don't know what the owner of Balanzategui can be thinking.'

Who knows what the lady of the house was thinking as she went back and forth in the living room upstairs and where she sometimes played music. She clearly wasn't thinking about grass, still less about what food would be best for us cows. It was obvious that she was as troubled as The Pest, although for different reasons, because the silences between one record and the next were broken by faint, unfamiliar noises: the sound of a door being slammed, or of a ladle being dropped on the floor. More than that, Stoopback had stayed in the house — we could see his bicycle in one corner of the barn — and was working in the attic. Why all this hustle and bustle? I wondered. But I had to wait until evening fell and it grew dark. The night would reveal the truth. The night not only brought out the moon and the stars, it also brought out other secrets.

It was black night when I heard steps. I couldn't see anything out of the little window opposite, but my ears immediately told me where those steps were coming from: they were light, elegant steps, very elegant, truly beautiful steps, the kind I had wished for myself at the moment of my birth. Yes, it was the sound of horse's hooves. The Pest can say what she likes about horses, that they don't sleep well and so on, but when it comes to the sound of their steps, they have no equal. No other creature walks like a horse.

The horses, five or six or possibly seven, stopped outside the barn, and then I could no longer hear their steps, but those of a party of men. Young, light-footed men, who, when they walked, barely touched the ground with their heels.

'It's all clear. Come on!' I heard someone say. It was Stoopback. The men greeted the old servant.

'How are things up in the hills? Were the paths all right?' asked Genoveva.

'The paths are fine, it's been a dry autumn,'

answered one of the men.

'The sooner we get the work done, the longer we'll have to eat. Let's set to, lads!'

'That's the trouble with this world, you have to work before you can eat, but, yes, we'd better get started,' joked the man who had spoken before, and the others all laughed with him. There must have been six or seven of them, but it was impossible to know who they were and what they looked like. Through the small barn window, I could see only the night and the occasional star. For her part, *La Vache qui Rit* was trying to peer through a crack in the barn door, but with little success. Given where we were, the only possible way of getting information was with our ears.

My ears told me that they spent about half an hour loading up the horses. What were they loading them up with? Well, judging from the noise made by one of the things when it fell, they were sacks, sacks full of something. But what? It was impossible to know. Ears have their limitations.

After loading up the horses, they all sat down to supper, but they ate quickly and spoke little. I could mostly hear Stoopback, who mentioned the word 'war' over and over: 'Serapio, the one who died in the war... after losing the war... the side that won the war...' But I still found it hard to pick up the thread of the conversation. *La Vache qui Rit* was also listening intently to the sounds coming from the living room, and she was the only other cow who was awake... this would be a good opportunity to make it up with her and start talking again. And yet I didn't dare go over to her. I thought she would be angry, that she would never forgive me for preferring the company of the stupid cows.

When supper was over, we again heard the light, elegant steps of the horses. They were so heavily laden that they found it hard to walk, but the sound was still very distinctive. At last, they set off back to the hills, and there was nothing else to do but sleep.

The following day, as soon as they opened the barn door, I went straight over to join the red cows.

'Who was here last night?' I asked Bidani. From the enclosure where they had spent the night, the whole front of the house was visible. It was, so to speak, a strategic viewing point.

'What do I care about who was here? I didn't see anything, but I slept wonderfully well,' Bidani said. At that moment, I made my decision: I would leave those stupid cows. Stupid cows are the most stupid thing in the world. Whatever it took, I would make my peace with *La Vache qui Rit*.

# Fifth Chapter

I DISTANCE MYSELF FROM THE STUPID COWS, AND, AS
A CONSEQUENCE, AM CAST OUT INTO THE DESERT. THE
CHEVROLET PICKUP TRUCK KEEPS BRINGING MORE AND
MORE FODDER. I DISCOVER ONE OF THE
SECRETS OF BALANZATEGUI.

Any cow who wants to be a proper cow and not a stupid cow will, inevitably, find herself in the desert; she will not achieve her heart's desire without first knowing that bitter realm, which, being far removed from this world, can offer her only sand. And among all that sand, without a blade of grass, without a drop of water, any cow who wants to be a proper cow will think she's going mad, and sometimes, on days when the sun beats down most fiercely, she will regret having set out on that journey and will dream of the good life in the barn she left behind. However, she, who well remembers how very stupid stupid cows can be, will not succumb to despair; she will carry on until she has crossed the desert and sees before her the lush green hills and the shady woods. Then, remembering the words of the poet, she will declare: *Cela s'est passé*, that's all over, I have emerged from hell, I see the world with new eyes and with renewed courage. I had no scales on which to weigh the value of things before, but now, in the desert, I have found it.

I, too, wanted to be a proper cow, to distance myself from stupidity as best I could, and to rejoin *La Vache qui Rit*, my first and only friend; but the path that led from the stupid cows to her was a path that crossed the desert. And the desert, in my case, had a name: Loneliness. Not Poverty, Illness or Prison, as so many other people's deserts have been called, but Loneliness. To put it another way, it was a desert entirely unlike Pauline Bernadette's desert, because hers was the one usually known as Matrimony.

'When I lived in Altzürükü,' she told me one day, 'I was happy and contented. I would spend all day in the hills, looking after my parents' cows, and with that and the prayers I said to God, I had all I could possibly want. But I grew and grew, and I became a very beautiful young woman, and then my father said: "You will have to get married, which means you must go to the Sunday dances." And I said: "No, I'm perfectly happy and contented taking care of the cows." And my father said: "No, from now on, you won't go to the hills any more, you will go to the dances instead, because you're a young lady now and must get married."

'That day, Mo, I entered hell, because I would go to the dances and all the boys would want to dance with me. And not only the boys from Altzürükü either, but the boys from Urdinarbe, Brissac, Ganges, Laroche and many other places. I didn't want to be with those boys, I wanted to be in the hills with my cows. One day, my father said to me: "Pauline, my dear, I can see how you hate having all these suitors, but you need suffer no more. Our neighbour Pierre has asked for your hand in marriage, and I have said Yes. He's a very good man, and he owns sixty cows and a lot of land."

'That was a very sad day for me, Mo. Before it had been hell, now it was hell and a half. I had spent five months unable to roam the hills with the cows, and the future was looking very dark. Pierre would come to the house every day: "My dear little Pauline," he would say, "when we get married, I will sell my cows and my land and we'll go to Paris and open a restaurant." I tell you, Mo, the first time I heard him talk about that restaurant in Paris, I fainted dead away. The next day, I said: "Pierre, I don't love you and I won't go to Paris to open a restaurant." And he said: 'Don't be so ridiculous, my dear little Pauline, I know you love me." And I said I didn't and he said I did. And then I locked myself in my bedroom and refused to come out. After that, Pierre would come every evening and stand under my balcony and sing. Finally, I decided to jump from the balcony and, may God forgive me, run away from home. And what happened then?'

'Well, you jumped from the balcony and landed on me. Fortunately, you were as light as a bird.'

'Yes, Mo, you're right. That's exactly what happened. You had just come from Altzürükü, and there you were under my balcony. I'm sure it was God who put you there, Mo. If it weren't for you, I wouldn't be here now in the convent. One day I must repay you for the favour you did me.'

'Oh, you've more than repaid your debt, Sister. Many times over,' I said, thinking of the clover and the fenugreek.

So Pauline Bernadette's desert was called Matrimony, and, as it turned out, it wasn't so very difficult to cross, she simply had to jump from a balcony, land on top of me and then enter the convent. My desert, Loneliness, seemed far drier and far bigger. On the one hand, I was determined to have nothing to do with the stupid cows in the barn: I would say hello to them, but nothing more. They could try to make conversation with me or offer me the best grass or nice places to rest in, but it would be no use. That was all over. On the other hand, my friendship with *La Vache qui Rit* had been badly damaged, and I had to let time take its course. I couldn't go over to the old mill and say: 'Here I am again. Tell me what Green Glasses and his big-toothed minions have been up to lately.' No, that was impossible. When you break off a friendship with someone, you have to do what Pauline Bernadette does with broken geranium stems: put that friendship in a fresh pot with some fresh soil and hope that it takes root.

Since I didn't want to be an ordinary cow, or to simply do nothing in the lonely weeks that awaited me, I started thinking about the problems at Balanzategui and set myself a task: 'Mo, you've already spent quite a time in this valley and yet you still don't know every corner of it,' I said. 'Why not explore the area? Why not go looking for the fallen aeroplane *La Vache qui Rit* told you about?'

I threw myself into this task with great enthusiasm, because that's the thing about the desert called Loneliness. At first, it doesn't seem too bad at all, and it's even rather pleasant, soothing and stimulating. While I went up hill and down dale in search of that plane, I felt better than I'd ever felt, and I congratulated myself on having rid myself of the stupid cows in the barn. Then, halfway through that autumn, I came to some rocks and saw the plane, and it seemed to me a good idea to stay there and think a little. And that's what I did. I settled down next to one of the broken wings and I thought about the war and about the pilot who had flown that metal machine through the air, and I thought, too, about how small the pilot must have been to fit in the cockpit... in fact, I thought about all kinds of things, because I wasn't in a hurry. It was a nice temperature, and the view from there — over almost the whole valley — couldn't have been better. What more did I need in order to live well? Nothing at all, I thought. As the saying goes:

BETTER A COW ALONE THAN A COW
IN BAD COMPANY.

Unfortunately, such happiness tends to occur only at the beginning, because, almost immediately, the worst enemy of those who have to cross the desert of Loneliness makes an appearance: Boredom. And that is precisely what happened to me, just as it had when I was trapped in the snow. I was bored with thinking. I was bored with kneeling there next to the plane. I was bored with talking to myself. And I began to look for new entertainments: one day, I went to the small cemetery in the wood and knelt down before the three crosses; the next day, I waited for the Chevrolet pickup truck bringing the sacks of fodder and raced it back to Balanzategui, as if it were a wager.

'Calm down, calm down!' the driver shouted, sticking his head out of the window. 'No one's going to steal your fodder!'

I wasn't interested in the fodder, of course, I was simply passing the time. Because that autumn, time barely passed at all, or passed so slowly that it gave me a headache. For my part, I continued to look for things to do.

'Mo,' I said to myself one afternoon that seemed even more interminable than all the other interminable afternoons. 'You haven't been to the old mill for a long time. Why not go and explore a little? You might be able to find out what Green Glasses and the large-toothed twins are up to there.'

I hadn't forgotten the fright those people had given me shortly after I was born, and this new plan of mine filled me with fear. The way things were, though, even danger seemed an attractive prospect. It would make the time pass more quickly.

My fears proved unfounded. The twins not only didn't recognise me, they didn't even appear to notice me. One of them was standing outside the main door to the mill, sitting on a white chair and reading a newspaper; the other one was at the new window that had been installed in the roof and — and this really was something new — peering through a long, fat telescope. There was no sign of Green Glasses anywhere.

'What's he looking at through that telescope? The valley? Balanzategui?'

I couldn't give a proper answer to that question. I had spent quite a long time feeling bored to death in the desert and — just as when I was waiting for the wolves to come in the snow — my brain was blocked, a stone slab stopped me thinking clearly. All I needed to reach a conclusion was to remember those horsemen who had ridden down to Balanzategui on the night of our banquet:

'The twins want to know when those men come down from the hills, which is why they're watching Balanzategui and the roads leading to it. They'll have a hard job though. The men from the hills always come under cover of darkness.'

I've only reached this conclusion since I've been writing these memoirs and knowing what I know now. That day, though, I hadn't a clue; any ideas I had lay crushed beneath the heavy slab of boredom. I took a walk around the mill and, having established that *La Vache qui Rit* wasn't there, I went back the way I had come. It would be about another five hours before it got dark. Those autumn days were really long!

Still deep in the desert, feeling ever more lonely and bored, I began to experience my first moments of weakness, and only my will and my capacity for suffering stopped me returning to the warmth of the barn, to its warmth and its music, because living as I was, far from the stupid cows, I never got to listen to Genoveva's records. Since I wasn't prepared to give one inch in my decision to be a proper cow, I devoted myself to finding new ways of passing the time, one of which was what I called 'The Game of the Leaves'.

This game consisted in guessing when a certain leaf would fall. I would go into the woods and, after finding a nice soft place to kneel, I would choose a leaf on a tree, a very green leaf, more like a spring leaf than an autumn one. Then, keeping my eyes fixed on the chosen leaf, I would stay there all day watching. Sometimes I would spend two or even three days, as long as it took. The leaves tended to take their time to jump off the branch into the air and from the air to the ground. Usually, a yellow spot would appear on the green leaf, then another bigger, yellower spot; not long after that, the leaf would turn completely yellow, apart from a small brown stain. When that brown stain spread, a few red dots would appear, which was a sure sign that the leaf was about to fall. And during that whole process, I would make bets with myself: 'I bet another stain will appear this afternoon and that the leaf will fall first thing tomorrow morning'. This game really helped me pass the time and forget my problems. And I sometimes had the great joy of guessing the exact moment when a leaf would fall.

This diversion was short-lived however. Winter was approaching, and the woods were growing ever barer. A few weeks later, when there wasn't a single leaf left to watch, I tried the same thing with branches, but that was no fun at all: either none fell or — when there was a storm — lots fell at the same time. I abandoned that game, and the stone slab of boredom once again fell on me.

One day, in the late afternoon it must have been, I saw a cow coming towards me. I didn't know who she was at first, but when she stopped next to a tree in front of me, I immediately recognised the large head of my old friend.

'It's *La Vache qui Rit*!' I cried, unable to suppress my joy.

I got up and went to meet her, but there was no one there.

'Where have you gone?' I cried. Then I realised what had happened. The cow I had thought was *La Vache qui Rit* wasn't a real cow, but an hallucination. Just as cows or camels in the Sahara or the Gobi and other deserts see mirages, and in those mirages see the things they most long for, a well or the shade of palm trees, so those lost in the desert of Loneliness think they see friends. That's what happened to me that day: I needed company, and my imagination did the rest, creating the ghost of *La Vache qui Rit*.

'My dear,' I heard a voice say inside me. It had been a long time since I'd had any contact with The Pest. 'I didn't want to say anything to you before, because I believe that in this important period of your life, which will certainly leave its mark, you need to struggle on alone and use your own resources. However, after all the difficulties you've been through, and bearing in mind that winter is fast approaching, I would like to suggest another way of passing the time, namely, study. Why don't you begin learning the names and the laws of the stars, my dear? It will come in very handy if you ever get lost in the hills. That red star up there, for example, is always the first to come out. As you see, it's still daylight, but there it is. Its name is Venus, also known as the morning or evening star.'

'So that's Venus,' I said, looking up and searching for that star in the sky.

'Or the morning or evening star…'

'Right.'

Venus or whatever it was called seemed a very interesting star to me. I stood there, gazing up at it.

'Later on, when it's dark, the other stars will come out. Above that mountain over there, for example, you'll see Andromeda and, next to it, Pegasus. As for the Pleiades, they'll appear on the other side of the sky. Orion and Sirius, for their part, will come out right here, immediately overhead.'

'So that's Venus,' I said to myself. The Pest couldn't interest me in the other stars. All my senses were focused on Venus. I watched that red dot to see if it would become redder, or if a yellow spot would appear, and I made bets with myself on how long or short a time it would be before it fell. This was as absurd as it was painful. I was in a very bad way. Loneliness had really done for me. My connection with the world was gradually growing weaker and weaker. Soon I would stop eating and drinking, and would stay there for ever, staring up at Venus like a statue.

What saved me was a whistle from Genoveva. The owner of the house was calling me, and she whistled again, louder this time, and, finally, one of those whistles managed to penetrate my brain and wake me up: yes, I was being summoned. Genoveva, she of the records, was calling me, it was winter, I was in Balanzategui. As soon as I started down the hill, I heard Stoopback shouting:

'Quick, all of you!'

Rapidly regaining my sense of self, I immediately remembered the banquet and everything that had happened on that other night: the horses coming down from the hills, the loading of the sacks, the conversation over supper about the war.

'Mo! Mo! Where is that stupid animal?' yelled Stoopback. I ran still faster and joined the other eleven cows outside the barn before he got really angry.

That summons and the banquet that followed were, for me, the first oasis I had found in the desert; there I could rest and screw up enough courage to continue my journey. As the poet said:

UNDER THE PALM TREES I DRANK,
UNDER THE PALM TREES I ATE,
WATER AND DATES TO RECOVER MY
STRENGTH.

I got my water and dates as soon as I approached Balanzategui. On the one hand, as I stood by the barn door, I heard the stupid cows muttering to each other: they were calling me arrogant and wild, comparing me with *La Vache qui Rit* and saying how I had changed. I took all these comments as compliments, and, a moment later, when Stoopback told us that the banquet was again for the black cows only, I entered the barn like a queen.

'Out of my way!' I told the red cows blocking my path, and they all obeyed without a murmur.

Happiness came not only from the reaction of the stupid cows, but from *La Vache qui Rit* too. She came over to my place in the barn and greeted me:

'How have you been getting on?'

'Fine,' I said.

'Excellent. I wonder what we're going to find out today. I have a feeling things are going to take a turn for the worse. We might yet hear rifle fire.'

'Let's talk later,' I replied, preferring to leave the door open for another occasion, and to break off our conversation there. Besides, I was too overcome by emotion to say or ask anything. I didn't even pay much heed to her dire warnings.

In the end, and despite my friend's misgivings, nothing unusual happened during that banquet.

It was exactly the same as the last time, down to the smallest detail. It was pitch-black night — with Pegasus, Sirius, Orion and all the other stars in their places — when we heard the elegant steps of the horses and Stoopback's words of greeting: 'It's all clear. Come on in.'

Then they loaded up the horses, had supper in Genoveva's dining room and returned to the hills. Given that everything was the same, The Pest again expressed her doubts: 'I still can't understand the behaviour of these people in Balanzategui. Why do they insist on providing us with fodder? With all the fine, tasty, nutritious grass out there, you'd think that would be enough. Why go to all this expense? I'd love to know how much each of those sacks costs.'

For my part, I thought: 'What is it they're loading onto the horses? They're sacks, yes, but full of what? Weapons perhaps? That's perfectly possible if, as *La Vache qui Rit* told me, the war isn't over in our valley. Whatever it is, it's obviously very important both for the people here in Balanzategui and for Green Glasses, because, of course, those sacks are the reason the big-toothed twins are watching the house through their telescope.'

'I don't think it can be weapons, my dear,' said

The Pest. She appeared to have been listening in to my thoughts. 'I didn't hear the clanking of weapons, not even when a sack fell from one of the horses.'

'That's true. It just made a dull thud.'

'We'll find out one day, my dear, but for now, it's best if you get some sleep. That fodder doesn't look very easy to digest, and so the sooner you get to sleep the better. Later, you might not be able to.'

We found out what was in the sacks much sooner than either The Pest or I could have imagined, because that winter — which was normally a very silent, monotonous season — turned out to be a time of great activity. It was as if the wheel of a big cart, which had been stuck in the mud until then, had finally extricated itself and begun turning. With each turn, that wheel — the Great Wheel of Secrets — began to spatter us with a little of the mud of truth, a mud that would, ultimately, take the form of what was really going on in our valley.

The visits by the Chevrolet pickup truck became more frequent, and, as a consequence, so did our banquets in the barn. And I'm right to say 'our', because all that winter, to the despair of the red cows, the banquets were nearly always for the black cows. During those banquets, it became the norm for *La Vache qui Rit* and me to talk. When we were outside the barn, we didn't talk at all, because that is what her wild boar's heart wanted, to be completely alone; but as soon as Genoveva whistled for us to go into the barn, we would start talking.

'It's the usual thing,' *La Vache qui Rit* said at one of the last of those winter banquets. 'As soon as there's no one at the mill, Genoveva calls us into the barn.'

'And now that there's no one watching, those horsemen will come down from the hills. I'd really like to know why, and why they give us fodder to eat when there's plenty of grass around,' I said, recalling The Pest's thoughts on the subject.

'If we had the answers to those questions, that would be an end to the secrets of Balanzategui,' she replied. 'But let's not say anything more just now,' she went on, as we were about to enter the barn. 'We have to be careful what we say with these fools listening. If they find out what's going on, they'll kick up a tremendous fuss. As you know, there's nothing in this world more stupid than a stupid cow.'

I looked at her and saw that special light in her eyes. She was a very proud cow with the heart of a wild boar. More than that, she was my friend again. Almost without realising it, I had walked across the last bit of desert and reached the other side.

*La Vache qui Rit* went to her corner of the barn and I to mine, waiting for darkness to fall on that winter afternoon. That was the cue for the men from the hills to arrive and load up their horses with those sacks containing who knows what. Perhaps we would be able to hear or see something that would help us get to the bottom of the mystery.

And, fortunately, that is precisely what happened. The Wheel of Secrets was already spinning in the mud, and some of that mud would spatter me with a fragment of the truth. It all happened before the horsemen arrived, when one of the cows — a rather unhappy black cow — came over to me and asked if she could share some of my fodder.

'Of course,' I said, 'but what's wrong? Have you eaten yours already?'

'No, I haven't, Mo,' she said, pulling a glum face. 'I don't like the fodder they've given me today at all. It's made up of small, hard white grains that get stuck under my tongue when I try to swallow them.'

'Really? Show me!'

I went over to her trough and saw that it was a kind of white fodder, the sort that men eat, not cows. In fact, it wasn't fodder at all, it was rice.

'May I eat some of yours, Mo?' the poor unhappy cow asked.

'Eat as much as you like,' I answered, barely able to contain my joy. I was sure that I had just made an important discovery, although quite why it was important I had no idea.

I decided to consult The Pest. I knew she thought I should learn things on my own and so on, and I still hadn't forgotten the air of unconcern she had adopted during that episode of the snow and the wolves, but this was a special moment. *La Vache qui Rit* and I were friends again, and I wanted to make her some kind of present. The meaning of that discovery, for example.

'My dear,' I heard her say, and I knew at once that she was going to grant my wish. 'The rice was in that nice cow's trough because someone made a mistake, that's all. That someone, Stoopback or even Genoveva, didn't realise what they were doing.'

'But where did that sack of rice come from? Why would they need so much rice in Balanzategui? For her and Stoopback?'

'I don't think so. Bear in mind that Stoopback nearly always goes home to the village for lunch. In my opinion, which will now be yours too, those men who come down from the hills take the rice back with them. That's why the sacks make that dull thud when dropped, because they're full of rice or something similar. I'll stop there, though, for I don't think I should say anything more. You're not a child now, and should start to think logically. Don't you see what's happening? In my opinion, it isn't exactly a hard nut to crack.'

I stayed where I was, not moving, trying to see the answer in the white rice in the trough. Almost at once, as if in a dream, I saw the Chevrolet pickup laden with sacks coming down the valley road to our house.

'The rice they take up to the hills comes in the pickup truck,' I thought, beginning to think very slowly and very logically. 'They disguise it by putting the sacks containing our fodder on top. If they didn't do that, the enemies of Balanzategui…'

I paused for a moment to take a breath. Thinking logically was exhausting.

'Go on, my dear, you're doing very well,' said The Pest encouragingly.

'The enemies of Balanzategui… Green Glasses and the twins! That's why Genoveva and Stoopback have to be so careful with those deliveries of rice. Otherwise…'

'We'd all be in a fine mess,' said The Pest.

'And on certain days,' I continued logically, feeling more and more exhausted, 'the men from the hills come down to fetch the sacks of rice. Then we get called in for the banquet, because, obviously, someone has to eat the fodder that has been used as a cover.'

'Very good, my dear,' said The Pest. 'That's the conclusion I reached too. As you know, I found all that unnecessary expense very strange. Why would Genoveva buy fodder when she has all the grass she could possibly want? Genoveva doesn't strike me as a bad manager. And she isn't, the money she spends on fodder is more than justified, because those sacks of fodder are crucial to the plan!'

'So this house…' I began again, taking my eyes off the white rice and looking over at *La Vache qui Rit*. My head was burning and I felt I couldn't possibly go on thinking so logically. However, The Pest didn't seem to want to finish my sentence for me. Or rather I was still being spattered by the mud from the Wheel of Secrets: there had been a war in the valley, they had shot Genoveva's husband, the war was not entirely over, Green Glasses was forcing the big-toothed twins to watch our house, the horses from the hills always arrived at night…

Finally, I collected up all those bits of spattered mud and made a little clay figure out of them, a sentence, a truth: 'Balanzategui is the storehouse for the army that has not yet surrendered!'

I couldn't go on. Thinking logically had drained me of all my energy and I fell asleep in front of the trough of rice.

After five or six hours, I opened my eyes and saw *La Vache qui Rit* beside me.

'Have you seen what's in here?' I asked.

'Yes, I know about the rice, but let's not rush into things. Did you find the place where the plane crashed?'

'Yes, I did.'

'Well, meet me there tomorrow at noon. We'll talk about all this then. Now, let's go back to sleep,' she said.

I was still exhausted, and it didn't take much for me to follow her orders. As the saying goes:

THE COW WHO THINKS A LOT SLEEPS
A LOT.

# Sixth Chapter

A long conversation between La Vache qui Rit and me. The Pest speaks to me about Alpha and Omega. The Great Wheel of Secrets begins to turn. Grave events in Balanzategui.

From the rocks where the plane had crashed we had a clear view of the valley of Balanzategui and the snowy hills round about.

'That's the good thing about this time of year,' I said to *La Vache qui Rit*, 'the woods are bare, and it's easier then to see the kind of world we live in.'

'And to see which cow is stupid and which is not,' she answered. 'Right now, the stupid cows of Balanzategui are in the barn, ruminating on what they ate yesterday and feeling too lethargic to go outside into the cold air. And the cold is so bracing! I've always said it and I always will: there's nothing in the world more stupid than a stupid cow!'

We were both kneeling down on the cold moss, she on one side of the plane and I on the other, chatting calmly to each other over the bits of rusted metal. We didn't want to launch straight into the subject that had brought us there. There would be time enough to ponder the discovery of the rice.

'I once had a most unfortunate experience in the snow,' I told her, letting myself be carried back into the past. 'There I was nibbling away at the short mountain grass and, before I knew it, a pack of wolves were following me. A bit of a shock, I can tell you.'

'Wolves? And how many did you kill with your horns?' said *La Vache qui Rit* raising her large head and with an eager look in her eyes. It was her wild inner voice speaking.

'Oh, I didn't kill any, but the one who was the leader of the pack went off toothless, because I dealt him a tremendous kick in the mouth.'

'Splendid! Well done!' said *La Vache qui Rit* enthusiastically.

'Of course, he went away with a prize too. He bit my tail.'

'Oh, that's nothing!'

*La Vache qui Rit* was staring now at the snowy slopes of the hills, wondering if the wolves were still there.

'What a shame I wasn't with you,' she sighed. 'I would love to have laid into those wolves myself! Where did you say you saw them?'

'On that long slope above Balanzategui, near the black rock.'

She stared over at the rock, and a shiver ran through her. Now and then, as if she were dreaming, she whispered the words dictated to her by her inner voice, words that were inevitably warlike: 'Get him! Yes, again! Stick it to him!'

'I'd have killed them all!' she sighed at last, before calming down and returning to her normal self.

'I'm sure you would,' I said.

'In a way, it's such a shame to have been born a cow!' she went on, turning to look at me. 'If we were like wild boar or like eagles, we would have to fight for our food, but, in exchange, we'd be free to go where we pleased. The mountains would be ours, so would all the mountain paths. No barn! No fodder! Entirely free, here today and gone tomorrow!'

'Listen, my dear,' I heard my Inner Voice say. 'Your friend is clearly an intelligent cow with a strong character, but, alongside those virtues, she has the grave defect of immaturity. What does she mean by saying that the wild boar enjoy total freedom? And what nonsense to say that eagles can do what they want, but we can't? Where are you now, for example? Aren't you precisely where you want to be? Can't you stay here for as long as you like? In short: do you really think the beasts of the hills are freer than you? Be serious, my dear. I don't think they are. I have nothing against the wild boar or the eagle, since they are both good, noble animals, but, to be honest, they are a bit limited. I would say that, on the scale of Alpha to Omega on which all living beings exist, they are very much Alpha. They have no barn, no place to find shelter. And they have no timetable for their meals, because they depend on hunting. Whereas you cows have it all. On the one hand, you have your freedom, and on the other, you have shelter and the kind of regular diet so essential to good health. In a word: the cow is definitely Omega and not Alpha. My dear, please understand this: we cows are special.'

'What's your Inner Voice saying to you?' asked *La Vache qui Rit*.

'That we cows are Omega, whereas the wild boar and the eagles have stayed pretty much Alpha.'

'Huh! Theories!' exclaimed *La Vache qui Rit*. And with a capacity for rational thought I had never noticed in her before, she went on: 'Your inner voice is a great one for philosophising, but it has no experience of real life. What does a wild boar care about being Alpha? A boar knows what really matters, namely, that the world is vast and that he can go anywhere he wants in that vast world: to the North, to the South, to the East or to the West.

That capacity to choose is what fills him with joy, a joy that slaves like us will never know. The wild boar may well be Alpha, but, in my opinion, he's far better than a cow.'

This was clearly his wild inner voice speaking. The Pest was beginning to grow impatient: 'Listen, my dear,' it said. 'Don't contradict her, because there's no point getting into an argument, but, then again, what does your friend know about the life of a wild boar? Absolutely nothing. And yet she speaks from the boar's point of view when she insults cows. I don't know, I really don't understand her. Perhaps she's going through a difficult patch. Anyway, you've been lying next to the wreckage of that plane for ages now and still haven't broached the subject. I haven't heard either of you say a word about what's going on in Balanzategui.'

The Pest was right about that. I, too, wanted to talk about Balanzategui, because, thanks to the pale sun that had just come out on that winter afternoon, I could see the telescope at the windmill, or, rather, I could see the lens glinting now and then. Whenever the toothy twins moved the telescope to face the sun, it was as if the mill gave off a kind of spark.

'Look, it's the twins,' I said to *La Vache qui Rit*.

'Yes, they're on guard. They're always on the

snoop to see if anyone visits Balanzategui.'

'What exactly do you think is going on here?' I asked, coming straight to the point.

'I told you before. The war that began in 1936 is not yet over. Not at least in our valley. The men who come down from the hills under cover of darkness don't want to surrender, and they're still at war with the General. And that's a very dangerous stance to take.'

'Is Green Glasses the General?' I asked innocently.

I may have slowly been gaining more common sense, but I was still in nappies as far as wars were concerned. I learned all those stories later, when I crossed the border and met Pauline Bernadette, because, during that other European war that took place in France, England, Germany and other places, the little nun worked for the Maquis, that is, for the French Resistance who refused to surrender to the Germans. I remember a priest coming to see her, a priest called Father Larzabal: 'Take these papers, Pauline,' he said, handing her a package. 'And this afternoon, lead your black cow along the mountain path to Altzürükü. The Maquis will know who you are and will come to meet you when they feel it's safe.'

The Mother Superior of the convent, who was standing nearby, frowned and said: 'I'm frightened, Père Larzabal! You're putting Sister Pauline Bernadette in great danger! There are soldiers posted all along the roads. If they search her, they'll take our petite Pauline prisoner.'

'Don't worry, Mother,' said Father Larzabal. 'Look at Pauline's face. And look at the cow's face. If the soldiers search anyone, it will be the cow.'

'But I don't want Mo to get hurt,' cried Pauline Bernadette.

'Don't worry, Pauline,' said Father Larzabal. 'You make a lovely couple, and nothing bad will happen to you.'

Things went just as the priest had said. The soldiers did carry out a cursory search on me, but not on the little nun, indeed, they hardly looked at her. And before we reached Altzürükü, she had placed the papers in the hands of the person they were intended for.

As I said, though, this was after everything that happened in Balanzategui, which is why I asked *La Vache qui Rit* that naïve question about whether Green Glasses was the General.

'No, of course not!' she said. 'Green Glasses or Knives is a hired killer sent by the General to pick off the rebels hiding near Balanzategui, but that's all he is, a hired killer.'

'Do you think Genoveva and Stoopback are heavily involved?'

'Definitely. They're at war too,' said *La Vache qui Rit*, speaking slowly and weighing every word. 'In Balanzategui, we cows are real cows and the grass is real grass, but nothing else is what it appears to be. To begin with, this isn't a farm or anything of the sort. It seems to be, but it isn't. As you've seen, there's no guard dog, and we cows do absolutely nothing. And there are no chickens or sheep or any other domestic animal. Worse, neither Stoopback nor Genoveva knows how to scythe grass.'

'That's very true,' I agreed.

'And then there's what we found out yesterday,' *La Vache qui Rit* went on. 'The truck doesn't come here to bring fodder for our banquets, but to bring rice for the men in the hills. That's what Balanzategui is for, it acts as a supply depot for them. Without Balanzategui, they would starve, and then the war would be over and so would everything else.'

'That's astonishing!' I cried, and I wasn't astonished by what she was telling me, because the same idea had occurred to me, but at how easy it was for her to think logically. She didn't seem in the least bit tired nor as if she were about to fall asleep.

'And what I want to know,' she said, sharper than ever, 'is why they can't just catch them? Why doesn't Knives or Green Glasses or whoever simply arrest the people in Balanzategui?'

'You mean the rebels who come down to Balanzategui, I suppose. Because putting Genoveva or Stoopback in prison would be pointless. It's the men in the hills they want,' I said.

'Yes, of course,' she agreed, 'but the question remains: why can't they catch them? There are the large-toothed twins with their telescope, spending all day snooping, watching for the slightest movement in the valley, and yet, on certain nights, the men come down on their horses, load them up, have supper upstairs, leave with their sacks of rice, and the hired killers know nothing about it.'

'The men in the hills must have some way of knowing which nights are safe,' I said, summoning up all my logical powers.

'Of course, but how?'

'Who knows?'

'Whatever the reason,' *La Vache qui Rit* went on in a grave voice, 'something bad is going to happen soon. As I said to you the other day, we're going to hear rifle fire in the valley again. Knives seems very irritable lately. Whenever he comes to the mill, he shouts at the twins.'

'Do you understand what he says?'

'After all the hours I've spent watching the mill, I understand him quite well now. Last week, for example, he talked about some act of sabotage. Apparently, the men from the hills blew up the railway line.'

'The railway line?' I said, surprised. At the time, I knew little about sabotage.

'Yes, they planted a bomb on the line. That's their way of carrying on the war.'

We remained silent for a while, staring at the rusting remains of the plane.

'Why can't they catch them, that's what I'd like to know,' said *La Vache qui Rit* with a thoughtful sigh. I nodded, because that's what puzzled me too.

However, we couldn't find an answer just then, not even with the help of logic. We would have to wait until the Great Wheel of Secrets began to turn again and spatter us with a little of that truthful mud. Only then, when we had enough mud in our hands, would we know what the reality was.

'Just wait a little, my dear,' I heard the voice say when *La Vache qui Rit* and I appeared to have finished our conversation. The Pest wanted to offer me her opinion. 'The mystery of Balanzategui can't be as indecipherable as it seems. It may be that your friend, being half-boar and half-cow, is incapable of reaching an acceptable conclusion, but you can. You're a cow from head to hoof, a cow, who, as she moves ever further up the scale from Alpha, is on the point of reaching Omega, and you're sure to clear up this mystery. Just wait a little, let the Great Wheel of Secrets give three more turns, and then think as logically as you can. And above all, *bon courage* and keep your head held high!'

The Pest was, of course, annoyed with *La Vache qui Rit*, but, all resentment aside, her opinion was as well-founded as ever. Later, everything happened exactly as she had predicted. The Great Wheel of Secrets turned three times, and, once I had applied my logic, the answer became clear.

The Wheel gave its first turn in the spring, when the trees were already full of green leaves. We heard Genoveva's whistle, her summons to the banquet, and the cows — *La Vache qui Rit*, me and the other ten — all gathered outside the barn. Contrary to what had become the norm at the time, the banquet that day was to be for the red cows, and not for us black cows. Stoopback began to prod us with a stick, telling us to move away from the house.

'Be off with you! Go to the pen!'

*La Vache qui Rit* and I looked at each other. We were finally going to be left outside, and so might see the men ride down from the hills on their horses.

The other black cows, who were too stupid to understand anything, insisted on trying to get into the barn, and Stoopback and Genoveva had a hard time herding them into the stone-walled pen. In the end, though, all seven of us were there. There, too, hiding in the grass, were all the creepy-crawlies that had arrived with the spring: mosquitoes, wasps, bees, worms, ants, snails, maggots, spiders, slugs, ladybirds, flies, horseflies, glow-worms, etc., all very Alpha creatures. And there, of course, were the flowers that always bloom in the spring, very yellow, very delicate, and very Alpha. Since I had the whole day ahead of me, I decided to squash a good number of creepy-crawlies and flowers, in other words, I knelt down.

'Let's see how many flowers I've squashed,' I thought after a while, and got up again. There were, in total, sixty-two, nine more than I'd thought. Neither good nor bad. An average result.

My wagers with myself didn't have the same purpose as they once had. This time, I wasn't struggling with boredom, but with nervous excitement. What would they be like, these rebels who continued to fight and refused to surrender to the General? And that question summed up all my anxieties.

By the time it grew dark, I'd already squashed about seven hundred flowers, then, suddenly, as if all the birds, all the leaves, all the dogs and everything else had been waiting for the signal to be quiet, the whole valley of Balanzategui fell silent. There wasn't even a sound coming from the house. Perhaps the only exception was the stream that continued to flow and to set the pebbles on its bed tumbling; however, that murmur was so similar to the silence that it didn't disturb it at all.

As for us, *La Vache qui Rit* and I were holding our breath, our eyes fixed on the path coming down from the hills. For a moment, the silence grew still deeper, like a hole growing bigger.

'Karral!' we heard suddenly.

*La Vache qui Rit* and I both looked round at the same time. Green Glasses was right beside the pen, brandishing his leather stick, and three guards armed with rifles appeared at his side and went and lay down near the house.

'Karral! Karral!'

About thirty guards, in groups of three, took

up positions around the house. Their rifles were all pointing at the path down from the hills.

'It's an ambush!' *La Vache qui Rit* whispered. 'They're going to catch the men from the hills. I told you we'd hear rifle fire in Balanzategui.'

'Not tonight, though, definitely not tonight!' I blurted out. This wasn't a conclusion reached by logic, it was merely a hunch. *La Vache qui Rit* stood looking at me, slightly perplexed, but not saying a word.

I don't know how long we waited, us and Green Glasses. It was quite a long time, most of the night in fact, but no one came down from the hills, and not a single light was lit in the house.

'Karral. Karral, karral,' said Green Glasses at last, addressing the very fat guard beside him.

'What's he saying?' I asked *La Vache qui Rit*.

'He says he can't understand why the men from the hills haven't appeared. I feel the same. I'm surprised too.'

'Karral!' bellowed Green Glasses.

'Karral!' repeated the fat guard even more loudly.

Shortly afterwards, the thirty guards who had been posted around the house were heading down the hill towards the stream. There they would find the path that crossed the valley to the village.

'You were right,' said *La Vache qui Rit* when Green Glasses and the fat guard had left. The night was just as dark as before and almost as silent. In addition to the murmur of the stream there was now the sound of thirty pairs of boots marching away. And yet that second murmur was also very similar to the silence and didn't disturb it either.

And that's how the events of the night ended, that and the first turn of the Wheel of Secrets. As The Pest had suggested, I decided to wait for the next two turns, not just playing dumb, but training myself up for the tremendous task of thinking logically.

The Wheel of Secrets was not the only wheel that knew how to turn, though; the Wheel of Time was also rolling on. The spring sun grew ever hotter, and the heat multiplied everything: where, before, you would see only one fly, one worm or one snail, now you would see and squash a hundred flies, a hundred worms or a hundred snails. Even the stream had undergone a transformation: it was full of rushing water covering the pebbles that had been dry for many months. On the other hand, there was less and less snow on the mountains and, finally, with the April rain, this disappeared completely.

On one of those rainy April days, *La Vache qui Rit* and I again heard Genoveva's whistle. The Wheel of Secrets was about to turn for a second time.

'It seems that today's banquet is going to be for us,' I said to *La Vache qui Rit*, when all the cows were gathered outside the barn. By then, Stoopback had already begun herding the red cows towards the pen.

'Perhaps today we'll find out something,' she responded as she went into the barn, whose doors, indeed, stood open for the black cows.

That night's visit was very brief. The six or seven men who came down from the hills took even less time than usual to load up their horses, and then, unusually, didn't stay for supper. When they were saying goodbye, Stoopback spoke to them very seriously:

'From now on, things are going to get difficult. Even sending you one more load of supplies will be hard. We're being watched all the time by that Otto fellow.'

'So Green Glasses' real name is Otto,' I thought to myself.

'How much do they know?' asked one of the men.

'They know you come down here, of course,

but they don't know how you avoid being seen by them, nor what you come here for. They think it's for weapons or documents. The other day, they stopped the Chevrolet truck and searched it thoroughly, but it didn't occur to them to look inside the sacks. The fodder for the cows was a very good idea. They were completely taken in.'

'So they're getting heartily fed up,' said another man.

'That Otto fellow certainly is. What infuriates him is that we always manage to get past his guards, but he hasn't yet worked out the system we have for communicating with you. He thinks we warn you by radio, but, like I say, this situation can't go on for much longer. We're being watched all the time. As you know, they've even put a telescope on the roof of the mill.'

'Oh, those wretched people at the mill! Those two treacherous brothers!' said a third man.

'Some day we'll get our own back, but now is not the moment. What matters is getting food supplies back to the battalion,' said Stoopback, speaking in a rather fatherly manner.

The men fell silent, and their silence helped us feel the other silence, the Great General Silence of the night. It felt as if everyone in the valley were sleeping, that the insects in the grass were sleeping, that the trout in the river were sleeping, that the foxes and the wild boar and the wolves in the mountains were sleeping. The owl was awake, of course, looking down at Balanzategui from a branch somewhere, but he was a very discreet bird and wouldn't go telling anyone about what he saw during his waking hours.

In the midst of that silence, I suddenly noticed the rushing waters of the stream, but the stream wasn't the only thing that was rushing violently on: the Wheel of Time was also speeding up, as was the Wheel of Secrets.

'When shall we come and pick up the last load?' asked the man who appeared to be the leader.

'The sooner the better, this week if possible,' said Stoopback. 'I've been listening to what people are saying in the village, and I found out that all the fascists are about to go off to Burgos, where they're apparently holding some kind of celebration. But, anyway, just keep your eyes peeled and watch for the signal. As I say, it will have to be soon.'

'Agreed. We'll be watching out,' said the leader, as if he were about to leave. The horses snorted impatiently and pawed the earth, but, as usual, they did so very elegantly.

146

'I'm so sorry we won't be able to send you any more supplies, but what can we do?' sighed Stoopback.

'Don't worry, Usandizaga,' said the leader.

'So Stoopback's name is Usandizaga,' I thought.

'Thanks to you, the battalion has eaten really well all this year. Everyone says the same, that the logistics corps has worked even better than when we were at the front. Besides, I don't think we'll stay in the hills for much longer. There's a rumour that we'll be crossing over into France.'

'We've done the best we could. Anyway, we'll see you again soon and work out whether we can get the last lot of supplies to you this week.'

'Give us the signal, and we'll be here, Usandizaga,' said the leader, who was already riding off.

From my stall, I looked across at *La Vache qui Rit*. Had she heard that? All Balanzategui's troubles would soon be over, and the war was finally coming to an end. But what was that signal both men had mentioned? There lay the nub of the matter. That's why they hadn't been caught, because they had a system of signals telling them if it was dangerous or not. But what was that system?

We would have to make ourselves think logically

and remain vigilant: the Great Wheel of Secrets was moving again, beginning its third and final turn, a turn which, moreover, would reveal to us the terrible reality that *La Vache qui Rit* had predicted. There would again be shooting in Balanzategui, and that man we called Stoopback — and whose real name was Usandizaga — would lose his life. For her part, Genoveva would go to prison. As for the cows — at least the fairly intelligent ones — we would finally understand the role we had played.

Three days after the conversation between Usandizaga and the leader of the battalion — on another misty April afternoon — Genoveva again summoned us with one of her characteristic whistles. The plan to send one last batch of supplies had been set in motion with the speed demanded by the circumstances. The work had to be done as soon as possible, while Green Glasses and the other killers were at the celebration in Burgos.

Once again, we black cows were herded into the barn. On this occasion, though, even the stupid cows didn't seem that interested in the fodder filling the troughs. There was something special in the air. My eyes and ears were very much on the alert: I saw the thick mist outside; I heard the piano music Genoveva had put on in the living room and the gentle trickle of water falling from our roof.

As the evening wore on, the record and the rain became intermingled until at last they seemed to form two sides of the same sound. Outside, the mist was taking on darker tones. In a couple of hours, night would fall on the valley of Balanzategui.

As soon as the first of those two hours began, rapid footsteps going up the stairs interrupted the dull silence in the house. The record stopped abruptly. Genoveva and Stoopback or Usandizaga, exchanged a few frantic whispered words, then came running down to the barn.

'Get out, cows! Get out!' Usandizaga shouted, while Genoveva opened the door. Both moved very quickly, especially Usandizaga. I looked at him: he was standing completely upright as he went from cow to cow, wielding his stick. He wasn't even that old. It was clear that, until then, he had only been pretending to be old and stoopbacked and full of aches and pains.

While Usandizaga herded the black cows towards the pen, Genoveva was bringing the red cows back to the barn. This was done very quickly, with the red cows in the barn and us in the pen. It was still daylight, and Usandizaga expressed his relief at this: 'At least it's still light, so I think we're safe,' he said to Genoveva. They were breathing heavily after all that rushing around.

'I bet Green Glasses will turn up later on,' I whispered to *La Vache qui Rit*.

And when night had fallen, he did turn up, warmly wrapped in his raincoat and brandishing his leather stick. As before, he ordered his thirty guards to take their positions around the house and watch the mountain path. Minutes later, everything was ready.

'Karral, karral,' said Green Glasses to the fat guard at his side. I thought I could hear a flicker of humour in the way he pronounced those words. He seemed to think that things were going to turn out well for them.

The fat guard merely nodded, and the valley again fell silent: the water trickling from the roof was the only sign of life. It fell and continued to fall. It fell, and the darkness grew. The water fell and so did time. Time was falling and continued to fall, and the darkness grew still darker. The misty spring night was drenching the roofs and filling the gutters with drops of rain, drops that would end up in the main gutter, drops that would fall in the form of that trickle of water, producing the only sound to be heard in the whole valley.

Green Glasses did not move from his post, he seemed to have dropped asleep standing up. In fact, he was wide awake, occasionally raising his leather stick and lightly tapping one of the stones in the wall around the pen. But no one came down the path from the hills. Not a sign, not a sound. Only the trickle of water from the roof, which fell and continued to fall as tirelessly as time itself. Finally, Green Glasses lost patience.

'Karral! Karral, karral!' he shouted, striking the wall with his stick. I'd almost drifted off to sleep, and his reaction startled me awake.

'What did he say?' I asked *La Vache qui Rit*, while my eyes remained fixed on the shadowy figure of Green Glasses. He was walking towards the house.

'He's saying something about how they must have a radio,' *La Vache qui Rit* said, with a look of incomprehension, because she could make no sense of his words.

'Green Glasses wanted to lay a trap for Usandizaga,' I explained. I'd spent some time thinking logically and was beginning to understand things. 'He spread the rumour in the village that he was going to Burgos and so on, and, at first, Usandizaga believed it. At the last moment, though, he realised it was a trick and told the men in the hills not to come. What Green Glasses can't understand is how he did that, what system he and Genoveva use to communicate. That's why he thinks they must have a radio.'

'Do they?' asked *La Vache qui Rit*.

'I don't believe so.'

I was right. The guards turned on all the lights in Balanzategui so as to search every corner of the house, and then used torches to do the same in the woods. In vain: in the corners of the house they found only dust, and in the corners of the woods only ants and spiders. Green Glasses was getting angrier and angrier.

'Karral!' he yelled at Genoveva and Usandizaga, who were now sitting on the bench on the porch. Usandizaga had recovered his former appearance: in the light from the bulb over the front door, he looked very old, a genuine hunchback. Genoveva, for her part, looked utterly blank and indifferent, staring out at the dark valley. What would she be feeling in that heart of hers that resembled one of our cow bells? I don't know for sure, but there was one moment when it did ring out: when the guards went over to the small cemetery and started searching among the crosses.

Hours after day had dawned, the thirty guards

were gathered together outside the house. They looked tired and hungry, waiting for the order to withdraw. But Green Glasses or Otto would not give up. Looking even paler than ever, he was pacing up and down the path to the hills. He was thinking as logically as possible. And I, too, was thinking as logically as possible.

Suddenly, on that grey April morning, his eyes and mine met, and his stick stopped twirling and remained poised in mid-air. I understood, and he understood. We both understood at the same time why they had never caught the men from the hills and how the people in Balanzategui communicated with them.

'Karral!' Green Glasses cried, his lips twisting into a smile. His stick cut through the air like a sword.

'Did he mention us?' I asked *La Vache qui Rit*.

'He did. He looked at us and said "the cows"!'

'That's the end of the story then. The men in the hills and the people here in Balanzategui are finished.'

'I told you something bad was about to happen, although I admit I didn't understand what was going on. I'm probably becoming stupid, which is terrible, because, as I always say, there's nothing in this world more stupid than a stupid cow!'

I reassured my friend. After all, she was intelligent enough to recognise that she hadn't understood. As the poet more or less said:

BETWEEN YOU AND ME, GOOD PEOPLE,
YOU NEED TO BE INTELLIGENT
TO KNOW THAT YOU'RE NOT.

Besides, I knew that her real problem was not a lack of intelligence, but her wild boar heart. She was less and less concerned about what was going on in Balanzategui. Whenever she was alone, her thoughts escaped to the icy mountains or the deep woods.

'Now they'll put us in the barn,' I said, seeing Green Glasses issuing orders.

'Us?'

'Yes, the black cows.'

And so it was. The guards rushed towards us and started to separate red cows from black, sending the black cows into the barn and the red ones into the pen. The only problem was *La Vache qui Rit*. She refused to budge, and the guards were keeping well clear of her horns. My friend's eyes were shining brightly, and I could almost hear what her inner voice would be telling her. 'Don't go into the barn, escape into the hills, crack open the head of that guard.' I looked at her, begging her not to do anything foolish, because if she didn't obey, one of the guards would shoot her. This was very bad advice, it must be said, typical of someone who over-estimates her own intelligence, because no one would have shot *La Vache qui Rit*. To do so would have sent a signal to the men in the hills that something strange was happening in Balanzategui. Anyway, that wasn't the only reason why *La Vache qui Rit* finally agreed to go into the barn; it had to do as well with the threatening movement made by Green Glasses.

'Karral!' he said, revealing the sword inside his leather stick.

A few other things happened, but, by midday, everything was as Green Glasses wanted it. The red cows were in the pen, and we black cows were in the barn. The guards were posted around the house and in the woods. Genoveva and Usandizaga were in the living room under careful watch.

'What's going on?' *La Vache qui Rit* asked when the barn doors were shut. She was staring at the trough before her. It was empty. There was no fodder that day.

'Let me explain in as few words as possible,' I began in a smug, arrogant tone, impressed by my own intelligence. 'Our question was how come they never caught the men from the hills, and that was precisely the question Green Glasses asked himself too. And the answer was that the people here in Balanzategui and the men in the hills must have some way of communicating between them. Otherwise, there was no explaining why it was that the men only came down on the days when the toothy twins weren't watching or didn't come down when they were...'

I paused for a moment to catch my breath. As usual, thinking logically wore me out.

'Go on,' said *La Vache qui Rit*. She wanted to know everything now.

'You see, the communication system consisted of two stages and still does. The first involved Stoopback or, rather, Usandizaga, because he's not stoopbacked at all... he just pretends to be a useless old man so that he can happily come and go between here and the village and get information, for example, that Green Glasses is going to be away, or that the twins have a wedding to attend, or whatever. That's how he and Genoveva knew when they were being watched and when they weren't.'

'And that's where we come in,' said *La Vache qui Rit*. I nodded and took the chance to kneel down.

Thinking logically really was exhausting.

'Exactly,' I said from my new position. 'Genoveva and Usandizaga would send the message via us. When we had a banquet, that is, when they put us into the barn for the whole day, the men in the hills would look down at Balanzategui and see that there were no black cows to be seen, only the red cows in the pen. And what did that mean? Well, it meant that if there were no black cows around, then Green Glasses and the other killers weren't around either, and it was safe to ride down and collect the sacks of rice. On the other hand, when they left us black cows outside, that sent the opposite message: "Be careful, danger, don't come down." On ordinary days, they let the red cows and the black cows mingle. With that simple system, the men in the hills were always kept in the know.'

*La Vache qui Rit* was looking at me wide-eyed. As for me, I was absolutely shattered. I was proud of my logic, but had now completely run out of steam and wanted only to sleep.

'And we're inside now,' *La Vache qui Rit* exclaimed, 'which means that the men in the hills will think it's safe to come down to get the rice. And Balanzategui is crawling with guards!'

'Precisely. Green Glasses has worked out how

the system operates and is using it in his favour. The men in the hills are doomed. They'll come down, and Green Glasses will kill them all.'

My breathing was getting slower and slower, and my head was drooping.

'No, not all of them. He'll need one or two to survive so that he can interrogate them later on about the rest of the battalion. That's what Green Glasses is after, not just a few men,' said *La Vache qui Rit*. She could think logically too.

After a moment's silence, I was about to open my mouth and explain to my friend that I needed a little nap, but as soon as I opened my mouth, my eyes closed and I fell deep asleep. And I remained asleep until, some hours later, I was woken by the bellowing of the cows.

I opened my eyes and saw through the barn window that it was now completely dark outside, and the cows around me were bellowing like crazy.

'The troughs are empty and they're hungry, that's why they're making such a racket. I'm hungry too.'

This was the key moment of that night. The noise we were making was like a stone hurled at a window, and when it hit the window, the glass — plain, smooth, transparent — would be shattered into a thousand pieces.

We were still bellowing when we heard shouts coming from upstairs in the living room. It was Green Glasses: 'Karral! Karral!'

'He's telling Usandizaga to make us shut up,' said *La Vache qui Rit*.

'He's afraid that the noise we're making will frighten off the men from the hills,' I said.

Moments later, we heard Green Glasses and Usandizaga coming down the stairs. Green Glasses moved rapidly and confidently; Usandizaga moved very slowly and painfully, still pretending to be a hunchbacked old man.

Usandizaga looked very pale when he came into the barn. At first, I thought he was about to speak to us, but he didn't even bother to keep up his pretence of being old and crippled. He ran to the corner where he kept his bike and grabbed a bag hanging from the handlebars. Within seconds, he had a rifle in his hands.

He raced out of the barn and up the stairs. He didn't stop in the living room though.

'He's going up onto the roof,' said *La Vache qui Rit*.

The stone was about to hit the glass. Usandizaga fired a shot from his position on the roof, and the silence of the night — plain, smooth, transparent — shattered into a thousand pieces. That shot echoed round the valley.

'It's a trap! It's a trap! Run!' Usandizaga yelled.

He fired another shot, and that second shot shattered any remaining fragment of silence — or glass. Green Glasses understood then that there was no other option and gave the order: 'Karral!'

The thirty guards all raised their rifles and fired at that other piece of glass shouting from the roof. By the time silence returned to the valley, Usandizaga was dead.

## Seventh Chapter

The situation at Balanzategui changes. *La Vache qui Rit* and I fall into the clutches of some young men. At a village fiesta, I recall the story of St Eutropio.

The same thirty guards who had killed Usandizaga also arrested and took away Genoveva, Balanzategui's owner, while we cows stayed alone at home. Initially, we all felt more at ease, because, on the one hand, it seemed that the war was finally over in our valley, and, on the other, we lived freely and weren't at the beck and call of some higher authority. It didn't take long, however, for most of my fellow cows to begin to grow nervous. They missed the banquets and the music, and kept asking after Genoveva. When would she return to the house?

Naturally, we couldn't answer that question with any exactitude, but even if we could have answered it, the problem was clearly a grave one. Genoveva would have to spend years in prison. Green Glasses himself had said as much after they shot Usandizaga.

'Karral! Karral, karral! Usandizaga karral!'

'He says Usandizaga was lucky, that Genoveva's fate will be far worse,' said *La Vache qui Rit*, translating. By then, all the black cows were out of the barn and grazing happily on the grass. We had managed to get ourselves released from there by sheer force of bellowing.

'Karral! Karral!' Green Glasses went on, brandishing his stick in Genoveva's face.

'She'll get a long sentence. She'll rot in prison,' said *La Vache qui Rit*, again translating.

Genoveva suddenly looked up and — after a long period of silence — she started talking. How long had it been since we'd heard Genoveva's voice? A long time. She was a very silent woman, the most silent woman I've ever known.

'You'll pay for this too, you murderer!' she screamed.

'Karral!' shouted Green Glasses, turning still paler, and two of the guards grabbed Genoveva and led her down to where a black car was waiting.

There we said goodbye to Genoveva, and from then on — once the happiness of those first moments had passed — the barn became a very anxious place. The stupid cows refused to accept that we'd said goodbye for ever to Genoveva, and kept asking about her. They missed the fodder;

they missed the music; they missed having someone telling them what to do, an authority figure.

'There really is nothing in this world more stupid than a stupid cow,' said *La Vache qui Rit* angrily. 'Now, when we finally have the chance to go where we like, all they do is complain and sigh. And why, when, at last, we have no masters! Isn't it better to be free?'

For all *La Vache qui Rit*'s angry words, though, the situation clearly couldn't continue like that. Most of the cows were simply not prepared to live their own lives.

'My dear,' said The Pest one day, 'you're quite right. The current situation is merely an interlude. They've taken Genoveva off to prison, possibly for a long time. And, at any moment, a new owner will arrive in Balanzategui. Best to keep your eyes open and not get caught up in mere daydreams like your friend.'

The Pest paused, then added, emphasising every syllable: 'Because the new owner could be Green Glasses.'

This comment knocked the breath out of me, as if I'd received a hard blow to the chest.

'But don't worry for the moment,' The Pest said.

'That's only a possibility. We'll see what happens. The Wheel of Secrets hasn't stopped turning, and will soon have turned enough for us to find out the name of the new owner.'

The days that followed this conversation with The Pest were days of great anxiety. I spent all my time looking at the road crossing the valley, and my heart beat faster whenever I saw someone coming. It was never Green Glasses, though. Sometimes, it was just a hunter or a passer-by; sometimes a local farmer returning from market.

One morning — it was May by then — I saw a small tractor leaving the road and heading towards Balanzategui. It was a shiny new red tractor, gleaming in the morning sun, and it brought with it two men. Two apparently young men. Two identical young men dressed the same and with the same hair. The Wheel of Secrets had clearly turned again: the large-toothed twins were the new owners of the house.

When the tractor stopped at the bridge over the stream, *La Vache qui Rit* began to protest: 'You've come the wrong way. Keep going! You live over at the mill!'

Ignoring her protests, one of the twins opened the gate that gave access to Balanzategui. In a matter of moments, the tractor was driving up towards our house.

'So the large-toothed twins have already received their reward!' exclaimed *La Vache qui Rit*, suddenly understanding what was happening.

'Yes, Green Glasses is rewarding them for services rendered,' I said.

'Let's get out of here,' *La Vache qui Rit* said, heading into the woods, and I immediately followed her. I wanted nothing to do with the new owners.

It became clear at once that the twins intended to squeeze every penny they could out of Balanzategui. They seemed to want to empty the place of everything: one day, they took away Genoveva's record-player; another day, it was a couple of mirror-fronted wardrobes; the next, the silver dinner service. And they didn't just plunder the house either, but the woods too, for they felled about forty trees and took away the wood. The tractor always left Balanzategui weighed down with stuff, and returned empty.

Nevertheless, their behaviour didn't bother us cows; we did as we pleased and had plenty of grass to eat. Indeed, because the April rains had been followed by bright sunshine the grass was more abundant than ever. Given the situation, I found it hard to follow the advice that The Pest kept on giving me: 'My dear, be careful! Keep away from the house!'

I didn't think this was necessary, but, just in case — and because I knew how far-sighted The Pest was — I never stayed in the barn. I usually spent my nights up in the hills with *La Vache qui Rit*, where we slept alongside the wreckage of the plane.

One day, I was looking down at the valley, when a thought occurred to me: 'Where is that silly cow Bidani? I haven't seen her for a whole week now?'

As soon as I said this, my eyes opened, and I felt my heart pounding.

'They're clearing out the barn!'

I looked again at the valley. There were two cows next to the stream. Another two were in the pen. Three were near the little cemetery in the woods. Seven cows altogether. With *La Vache qui Rit*, eight. And with me, nine.

A shiver ran down my spine. Death was on the prowl in Balanzategui. Bidani and another two red cows had felt the cold steel of the knife.

Even though it was quite a hot day, I couldn't stop shivering. Suddenly, even the woods didn't seem like a safe place. I got up and ran over to *La*

*Vache qui Rit.*

'Yes, I know,' she said. 'But don't worry, they won't catch us. We're not like those other stupid cows.'

I wasn't so sure, and I found it hard to regain my composure. I decided to take The Pest's words of warning to heart: 'Be careful! Keep away from the house!'

Some time later — it would have been summer by then — we heard a few small explosions in the valley.

'What's that?' I asked *La Vache qui Rit.*

'Oh, it's nothing. There must be a fiesta going on in one of the villages nearby.'

'A fiesta?' I said, surprised. I had never heard the word before.

'That's what they call it. And whenever they hold a fiesta they send up those rockets, but that's all I know. I've never been to one.'

'I'd love to go to a fiesta!' I said innocently. I was still very young and foolish, and had no qualms about expressing such a wish. Unfortunately, my wish was soon granted.

It happened a few weeks later, in the hottest part of the summer. The grass, which was already pretty dry, had turned really sour, and the springs

— which were already fairly depleted — had dried up altogether. *La Vache qui Rit* and I were thus confronted by two problems, one serious and one really serious. The serious problem was not being able to eat as much as we should like. The really serious problem was that there was nothing to drink.

The only solution was to go down to the stream, or, to be more exact, to the pool beneath the bridge in Balanzategui. There was a little fresh grass there, and, more importantly, water.

One day, we were underneath the bridge drinking, when we saw three young men coming along the path. They were chatting and laughing, and didn't appear to be dangerous. Appearances, however, can be deceptive, because when they were close enough, and completely without warning, they threw a thick rope first around *La Vache*'s neck and then around mine.

'What's going on?' I thought and I felt frightened. Meanwhile, *La Vache qui Rit* was shaking her head, trying to free herself from the rope, but without success. We had fallen into a trap.

At first, we refused to come out from under the bridge, but had no success there either. The young men soon put paid to any resistance. They just had to poke us with some pointed sticks called goads. A couple of prods was enough to get us onto the bridge, because being poked with a goad really hurts.

As soon as we were there, we saw the two large-toothed twins coming towards us. I looked up and saw that the sky was blue; I listened and heard the crickets singing; I imagined what was about to happen to us, and realised that *La Vache qui Rit* and I were at the gates of death.

'The two of them are practically wild and will certainly give you a run for your money. They'll be far better than any bulls,' one of the twins said to the young men.

'Are you sure?' asked one young man.

'Absolutely. The ugly one, Bighead we call her, she's really ferocious. She'll attack anyone.'

I haven't ever mentioned this before, but I will now. My friend hated her real name, Bighead, which is why she had adopted the name *La Vache qui Rit*. She herself told me about that change shortly before we parted for ever: 'Once, when Genoveva's husband was still alive, a French family came to visit. And for some reason, one of their children started calling me *La Vache qui Rit*. One day passed, and then another, and still he insisted on calling me *La Vache qui Rit.* I liked the sound of the name and decided to keep it and get rid of the other ugly name I'd been given. It was that little French boy who christened me. And the day has come when no one can call me Bighead ever again. Anyone who does will live to regret it.'

As the twin who had called her by that name soon found out, this was no empty threat. When the young man holding the rope wasn't looking, *La Vache* hurled herself at the twin and caught him in the leg, tearing his trousers. And she would have done far worse if the other young men hadn't intervened.

'Now we've really gone and done it,' I thought, believing that they would kill us right there and then.

In fact, the opposite happened. Both the twins and the young men seemed happy and contented.

'Didn't I tell you? These cows are ferocious, and will definitely give you a run for your money. It will cost you, though. If you want quality, you have to pay for it.'

'How much?' asked the young men.

'This much,' said one of the twins. I can't remember the exact amount now, but it must have been a lot, because the young men protested.

'You can protest all you like, but I'm not going to lower the price one penny. They're quality stuff these cows, ideal for any fiesta. If you don't take them, I'll sell them to someone else.'

'So they want us for a fiesta,' I thought, feeling reassured. I had no idea then what awaited us.

'All right, we'll take them,' said the young men, giving in. They got out their money and paid the toothy twins.

'Come on, you two!' they cried and we all set off. For the first time in my life, I was going to a fiesta.

I won't describe everything that happened to us in the village. I couldn't even if I wanted to, because what I experienced and learned there would fill a whole encyclopaedia and more. That said, I won't tell everything I could tell either. After all, why drag the thing out by piling detail upon detail, when the truth can be summed up in one sentence, which is, more or less, what happens with the truth about the people in that village and their fiestas. And the truth is this: whenever I think of them, I gather a nice gob of saliva in my mouth and then I spit — hard. Enough said.

However, since I am writing my memoirs, I will try to say a little more. And to help me, I will tell one of Pauline Bernadette's stories.

Pauline Bernadette is always telling me stories, usually stories about saints. For example, one day, we were outside the door to the convent — I was kneeling on the grass and she was sitting in the shade sewing — when the baker arrived, bringing some bread for the nuns, and Pauline Bernadette said: 'Oh, look, Mo, it's the baker. And yet, that's a shame too. I wish the same thing would happen to us as happened to Paul the Anchorite. The saint spent sixty years all alone in the desert, and every day a crow would bring him half a loaf of bread. One day, after he'd been there for sixty years, St Simon visited him. And what do you think happened? The crow brought a whole loaf. A double ration! Ah, those were the days! They didn't need bakers!'

'Bakers have to make a living too, though,' I said, looking at the man unloading his loaves.

'That's very true, Mo. It's just as well that Our Lord doesn't perform miracles any more, well, he does in Lourdes, of course, but he still leaves work for the doctors to do.'

However, this isn't the story I meant to tell, but another one she told me when we were looking at some milk churns.

'Don't they look splendid in the sun, those

lovely clean churns!' she cried. 'How they shine!'

I nodded. I do try and agree with her whenever possible.

'I look at those churns, and I remember what happened to St Eutropius, Mo. Do you want me to tell you?'

Again I nodded.

'Well, apparently, Eutropius was a musician, known throughout the region for his fine musical ear. One day, the wicked emperor ruling the country took him prisoner and said to Eutropius: "So you still insist on belonging to that other religion, do you? We don't need the Christian faith here!" And Eutropius replied: "I am a Christian and I will not deny my religion." "So you won't deny it," said the emperor, laughing. "We'll see about that!" And the emperor gave orders for Eutropius to be put inside a really, really big milk churn, as big as a wine vat, and left him in there. "I wonder if they're going to cook me?" thought Eutropius eagerly, because his faith was very strong. But they didn't cook him. The emperor wanted to damage that fine musical ear of his, and, after having the churn placed in the middle of the main square, he published an edict: the man who could hit the churn hardest would be given a large reward. So, of course, many people stepped up, hoping to get the reward, because people then liked money too, just as they do today. One man used a hammer, another a mallet, someone else a stone, and they all struck the churn again and again and again. You can imagine the racket they made with those blows, and for two or three days no one in that city slept, not even the emperor. And what about Eutropius? Well, an angel appeared to Eutropius inside the churn, and covered the saint's ears with his soft hands. And Eutropius remained in that sweet state of deafness all the time he was kept in the churn. When the lid of the churn was removed, everyone was amazed to hear Eutropius say: "Thank you very much. This churn is an excellent place to get a good night's sleep." Imagine! There he was stuck inside the churn, and he was the only one to get any rest.'

That was the story I meant to retell as the best way of describing how *La Vache qui Rit* and I felt at the fiesta, because being plunged into that fiesta was like being put inside a milk churn with no hope of any angel appearing.

From the pen where the young men imprisoned us, all we could hear at first was the buzz of people talking in the square and in the street. The buzzing resembled dust, making the air thick with noise.

There must have been thousands of people all talking at once.

'Why do they have to talk so much?' I said to *La Vache qui Rit* rather irritably.

'They're probably all drunk,' said *La Vache qui Rit* scornfully. Her eyes were very bright.

Just then, above the buzzing crowd, we heard the blare of strident music. It was obviously a brass band, a brass band which — equally obviously — was coming ever closer. Shortly afterwards, hammers, mallets and sticks began beating on our churn. There were clarinets, trumpets, and, above all, the bass drum, so loud that my friend and I couldn't hear each other speak. The music was crushing our words.

*La Vache qui Rit*, who was always more highly strung than I was, kicked the door. Not that this did any good, because the door was very solid. She did, though, make a hole through which someone — just to make our situation absolutely clear — slipped a firecracker, which immediately went off, and the noise of the explosion echoed around inside our heads.

That explosion was immediately followed by the beating of the bass drum. The drummer, who was probably the strongest man in the band, insisted on performing a solo, hitting his drum again and again, one-two-boom, one-two-boom, and so on for ten, twenty, forty minutes. He appeared to be inexhaustible, hypnotised by his own one-two-boom, one-two-boom. You didn't need to have as fine an ear as Eutropius to end up pounding the walls. And that is what we did, we kicked at the walls in order to harm ourselves and so forget for a moment that one-two-boom. The band's strong man didn't care, he tirelessly continued his one-two-boom, one-two-boom. By the time they opened the doors of the pen, we were both very nearly mad.

The doors of the pen opened, and it felt as if someone had taken the lid off the milk churn; the noise continued, but at least we could breathe. *La Vache qui Rit* shot out of the pen with one clear objective: she barged past the people crowded round the door and launched herself at the drummer, leaving the wretch writhing in pain, his ribs well and truly broken, and, I imagine, with little desire to continue beating his drum.

At first, we did pretty well and dealt some good blows, well, mine were good, but *La Vache qui Rit*'s were even better, and if I can now boast of being a cow who has broken more than thirty bones, I can do so largely because of that fiesta. There were a lot of people in that village, though, and they swarmed around us like horseflies. After half an hour of fighting and running up and down the main street, we both started looking for a way out. But where? Both the square and the street were blocked by a metal fence, and the people watching formed a second fence. We were inside a milk churn with no holes and no cracks.

Gradually, tiredness got the better of us, and we began to grow demoralised. The young men of the village were all excited now, and treated us with less and less respect. When one of them grabbed me by the tail, I knew that all was lost. I looked at *La Vache qui Rit*, and she was in no better state than I was. On the contrary, she seemed even wearier and closer to madness.

I told myself that anything was better than just giving up like sheep, and I kept looking for a way out. I came to a house I'd noticed before. It had a large gate that opened onto another street. As a way of escape, though, this proved to be both utterly futile and the lowest point of the fiesta. I was about to batter down the gate when I felt a sharp metal point pierce my flesh. Blind with pain, I spun round; this, too, proved futile, because my horns caught the bars on a low window.

'Karral!' I heard then. On the other side of the window was Green Glasses, smiling his twisted smile.

I felt like dying right there and then, but the young village drunks weren't ready to let me die. Every time I threw myself to the ground, they would force me to my feet and drag me after them. At one point, I saw *La Vache qui Rit* ahead of me, surrounded by people and gasping for air: she, too, was covered in blood; she, too, had felt the point of Green Glasses' steel dagger.

I can barely remember what happened next. I could hardly stand. Fortunately, just to make us look still more ridiculous, those vile people shoved us into the fountain. And I say 'fortunately', because not only did the cool water revive us, we also spotted a way out in the form of a pile of logs, which, quite accidentally, formed some rough steps that led up to the top of the wall surrounding the square. We only had to climb that rustic staircase, jump over onto the other side and be free.

'Do you see that?' I said to *La Vache qui Rit*.

'Yes. It's our only hope,' she said.

We were still marooned there when the young men who had brought us to the village reappeared. They hauled us out of the fountain and, after putting a rope around our necks, led us back to the pen.

'Oh, don't put them back in there just yet!' shouted one of the drunks.

'Don't worry, we'll let them out again tonight,' came the answer.

*La Vache qui Rit* and I spent hours kneeling and licking our wounds. At last, when, at supper time, the milk churn grew slightly quieter, we discussed our escape.

'We have to use our little remaining strength to reach those logs. We have to escape as soon as possible, otherwise, we're lost.'

'But when do we get to crack open the head of that Knives fellow? When?' she said in reply, although this wasn't exactly a reply, more of a lament.

'Maybe one day,' I said. There was no alternative. If we wanted to get out of there alive, we had to forget about Green Glasses.

We fell silent again, each of us immersed in our own thoughts.

'But when do we get to crack open the head of that Knives fellow?' *La Vache qui Rit* would murmur every now and then.

Towards midnight, the buzz of voices returned, and *La Vache qui Rit* and I prepared ourselves. We weren't afraid, our minds were fixed on our one objective.

We took everyone completely by surprise. We didn't respond to any attack or react to any challenge. We headed straight for the logs, and with one bound, we were out of the milk churn. Moments later, we were running for all we were worth.

# EIGHTH CHAPTER

*LA VACHE QUI RIT* AND I BEGIN LIVING UP IN THE HILLS
AND SEE SOME WILD BOAR. THE PROBLEMS THAT ARISE
BETWEEN US, OR HOW WE PARTED. I HAVE A SERIOUS
CONVERSATION WITH THE PEST ABOUT INDIA, PAKISTAN
AND OTHER PLACES ON THE PLANET.

After escaping from the village we simply ran, in no particular direction, our sole objective being to put some miles between ourselves and those horrible people at the fiesta. However, once we were far enough away and could no longer hear their shouts, we didn't know quite where to go. We certainly didn't want to return to Balanzategui, but could think of no other possibility.

'Let's head for the hills!' said *La Vache qui Rit* after we'd been walking for several hours and were both exhausted.

'Agreed! And let's do that now. We can rest once we're sure we're safe,' I said.

We started running again, more enthusiastically this time, but with little success. It was hard to find a decent path. Almost all paths led up a hill and then, when we least expected it, changed direction and started to head back down into the valley again. This was a real problem: we wasted what little energy we had and wasted time too, especially the hours of darkness that were particularly precious for two fugitives like us.

When we were both tired and fed up with all those false trails, I heard the voice of The Pest saying:

'Listen, my dear, you're going about this the wrong way. You keep looking for a good broad path, but that will never take you up into the hills. To get into the hills, you have to choose the bad paths.'

The Pest spoke very kindly, perhaps because she was still shocked by what had happened to us at the fiesta. Having said that, I would like to mention something else. And I will. And it's this: whenever I talk about The Pest, I tend to do so rather sourly, because she's always bothering me and won't leave me alone. And it's true that my Voice, my Guardian Angel or whatever, does talk too much and is always a terrible know-it-all, but I have to admit that she has always been a very good and intelligent friend to me. Very intelligent and very astute. And faithful too. And that's all I have to say. But I couldn't conclude these memoirs without mentioning her many good points, and now I have. Anyway, let's go back to what she taught me that night.

'Sorry, I don't understand. What do you mean "bad paths"? What bad paths?'

The Pest sighed deeply — or so I thought — then went on: 'Look, my dear. The paths near the village are broad and smooth, but they get narrower on the outskirts, and not only do they grow narrower, they even disappear altogether after knocking at the door of the last house in the village. Do they all disappear, though? No, my dear, not all of them. Some continue on up towards some solitary house in the mountains, getting narrower and narrower and narrower. So narrow that most disappear before they even reach that solitary house. Most, I say, because there are always some paths that carry on to the very top or to some high woods, breaking off here and there and becoming instead only a faint track. In the end, that track vanishes completely too and becomes part of the wood or merges with the rocks at the top. And that is where the real hills are, my dear. That is the part of the world with no paths at all.'

Even before she had finished speaking, I knew The Pest was right. And *La Vache qui Rit* agreed.

'Of course! How stupid of us. There really is nothing in this world more stupid than a stupid cow. Let's go in search of one of those bad paths!'

The first one we found led us to a small rural settlement, and the second to a house built on a slope planted with fruit trees. The third fairly narrow, stony path took us into a small wood that provided us with a place to rest for a couple of hours. Then, following yet another track, we came to a small rocky plateau. By then, it was getting light, and all we could see were mountains: four to the right, two to the left, seven ahead of us, and five behind us. Eighteen peaks altogether. Not a single house or hamlet or village. We were definitely out in the wilds.

'Now we're free!' cried *La Vache qui Rit* cheerily, forget-ting her tiredness and her wounds. 'There are no paths around us, which means that all possible paths are ours. Why don't we go and explore that peak over there tomorrow?'

'Tomorrow? Why not the day after?' I said, feeling in need of a rest.

Before I had even finished speaking, *La Vache qui Rit* was on her feet, her head raised. A shudder ran through her entire body, and her yearning gaze was fixed on the peak she had just mentioned. I followed her gaze and saw five wild boar running through the undergrowth. They were in formation, all in a line, like five brothers.

'Wild boar!' shouted *La Vache qui Rit*, breathing

hard. I could almost hear her heart pounding.

*La Vache qui Rit* remained silent and motionless for quite a while. Even though the boar had now disappeared from view, and even though the sun was beating down and making our wounds sting, she stayed there, her eyes fixed on the undergrowth. When she came to, she said abruptly: 'What do you mean, the day after? No, we'll go tomorrow!'

I was too tired to argue, and I didn't want us to quarrel on this our first day. And so I said nothing. And yet I already had a suspicion that we would eventually fall out with each other. And I've never liked being spoken to sharply.

When you live up in the mountains, there's very little to do. As a cow in a barn would say, there's absolutely nothing and no way of passing the time. Life there is rather like having to make a fire out of one pathetic bit of kindling. And who knows, perhaps that argument is perfectly logical and reasonable, because, after all, normal cows have thousands of things to do: one day, they're driven off somewhere in a truck; another day, they have a visit from the vet; the next, the owner of the house asks them to try out a special kind of fodder. And then there are the visitors, the music, the work… in short, for barn cows, kindling is a thing of the past, for they have whole logs with which to start the fire of life. The question is this: Is the big fire made from those logs necessarily better than the small fire made from kindling? I don't think so. I clearly remember something Pauline once told me, and which will help us clarify the matter: 'That year, the winter dragged on for a long time,' she said, 'and we ran out of wood to light the fire in the refectory. So I went out looking for branches and twigs along the sides of the road, to see if we could get by with those bits of wood until the end of winter. On one of the last really cold days, I came across a miserable little black twig, which looked as if it had been burned already, and for a moment I hesitated: "Shall I pick it up or shan't I?" And what do you think happened, Mo? Well, I put that ugly, miserable little twig on the fire and out of it sprang all kinds of brightly coloured flames. For example, one flame was light blue, the same colour as the cloak on the statue of Our Lady in the chapel; another was like a golden tongue; and a third was a kind of pearly green. And there were other flames, too, all mingling together. Really beautiful. I tell you, Mo, I've never seen a fire like it. I was so transfixed, I forgot to eat. So you see, Mo, the ugliest, most wretched things can conceal marvels.'

What Pauline Bernadette said to me then was very true, as I found out during those months spent in the mountains. At first, time passed very slowly, and I tried to spend most of my day sleeping in some cosy corner. I certainly didn't regret going there, because I still couldn't forget what we had suffered in Balanzategui, but my new home seemed very dull in comparison: no stream, no maize field, not a single orchard. Had it not been for *La Vache qui Rit*, I don't know what would have become of me in those first few months. I might have fallen ill with boredom, just as I did when I cut myself off from the stupid cows in the barn. But, as I say, I had *La Vache qui Rit*, or as the poet says: *J'avais une copine*, I had a friend.

However, by the time summer was over and the gentle September sun had arrived, I had already begun to see the bright, colourful flames of a new way of life. And like Pauline Bernadette, I was transfixed by that miniature blaze. The days passed without my even noticing: it was as if, once free of obstacles, the Wheel of Time had started to turn easily. And autumn was followed by winter, and winter by spring and spring by summer again.

'We've been here for a whole year now,' I thought one day, noticing that the sun was once again beating down. I was surprised by this thought. A whole year? And what had I done in that year? I didn't know then, and I don't know now. As the saying goes:

A CONTENTED COW HAS NO TALES
TO TELL.

And that's how it is with that period of my life: I remember only that I was happy and that memory floats in my mind like a cloud. What I do remember was that we spent most of the days exploring.

'Why don't we go and explore that big forest?' one of us would say, and off we would trot. Naturally, we didn't trot as elegantly as a horse, but certainly better than any other cow. And the secret of our happiness lay in that trotting, vagabond life.

Careful, though! Let's stop right there and tell the whole truth and not turn into another Pest, who is always smoothing away rough edges and rounding off any awkward corners. I'm going to correct what I wrote in the previous paragraphs. I've made it sound like *La Vache qui Rit* and I were happy, and I need to qualify that statement, only qualify, mind, not change it.

Not all the flames of our life in the mountains were brightly coloured — there were also a few black flames. And this was always, without exception, because of the wild boar. Whenever those five brothers ran past, *La Vache qui Rit* would do exactly as she had on the day we arrived: first, she would stand stockstill and trembling as if hypnotised, then she would turn on me with some brusque, rude comment.

I knew exactly what was happening. Two voices were doing battle inside her: one was telling her to continue being what she was, and the other — that aggressive inner voice — was telling her the opposite, that she should stop being a cow and join the wild boar.

It must have been very hard for her to keep her sanity, and *La Vache qui Rit* did her best and more to remain by my side. I understood this perfectly. Had I been in the same situation, who knows how I would have behaved, probably worse than she did. But regardless of whether I understood or not, the black flames were still there and growing worse and blacker with each day that passed. At any moment, morning, evening or night, she would suddenly turn sulky and surly.

Since we were friends, I ignored it and said nothing, but things couldn't carry on like that. After all, it wasn't right, it wasn't fair, because I had to pay a price for our friendship that she did not. I asked for nothing in exchange for her friendship, except that she be my friend. She, on the other hand, not only required me to be her friend, she also required me to be excessively humble, because in order to put up with her insolence without complaint, I had to be very humble indeed.

*La Vache qui Rit* and I separated in two stages, or to put it another way, it took two tugs to pull us apart. The first tug occurred in Balanzategui, the second and last occurred during a snowstorm, when we were looking for a cave to shelter in. Then, after all that time together, we did finally separate for ever.

The Balanzategui incident took place in the autumn. A south wind was blowing, and we both felt an urge to revisit our birthplace. And so we set off to Balanzategui and, by noon, were already gazing down at our valley from our old observation point: the rocks where the plane had crashed.

'There are new people living in the house,' I said to *La Vache qui Rit*, indicating some women sitting on the porch. From that distance, I couldn't recognise any of them.

'The twins don't seem to be around,' she added pensively. She still hadn't forgotten what had happened at the fiesta.

'Who knows where they might be living now,' I said.

'Somewhere nice, I bet. They could take their pick of houses from the sale of all those stolen goods. There's hardly anything left of the woods.'

This was true. The woods where we'd been born had been decimated, and the only remaining trees were those near the little cemetery with the three crosses. From my point of view, though, this wasn't the worst thing. The worst thing was that there wasn't a cow to be seen. The pastures were completely deserted. The lives of our old companions had been sacrificed to the greed of those large-toothed twins.

'Oh, what does that matter?!' said *La Vache qui Rit* suddenly. 'What does it matter what happened to those stupid cows! They deserved it!'

'That's what you think,' I said abruptly. I'd let her get away with a thousand and one other remarks, but that comment about our former companions seemed to me outrageous.

'Yes, it is!'

'Well, I completely disagree!'

'Of course you do, since you yourself are borderline stupid!' she yelled.

'That's rich coming from you!' I bellowed back,

turning on her, ready to attack.

For a few moments, we stood there, face to face, as if we were about to come to blows. However, we'd been friends for far too long to behave in such a shameful manner.

'We'd best get back to our home territory,' said *La Vache qui Rit*.

'Yes, that would be best,' I said.

From then on, throughout the autumn, she didn't address a single sharp remark to me. Instead, she would remain silent for hours at a time, and on some nights, without a word, she would leave our usual resting-place. Where did she go? To join the wild boar of course. Her inner struggle was growing ever more intense. It would not be long before she made a final decision. She had to choose one side or the other and she made her choice that same winter. *La Vache qui Rit* would join the herd of wild boar, and our friendship would come to an end.

It happened one very cold day when we were trying to take shelter inside a cave. As soon as we entered, I realised that someone else had got there before us, that another animal had taken refuge there. I peered into the darkness, and there I saw the same five boar we often saw running in a line.

'What shall we do?' I asked *La Vache qui Rit*. Two

of the boar had stood up in a threatening manner.

'Tell me. What shall we do?' I said again when she didn't reply. I wanted an answer, to know if we were going to fight for the cave or not.

'You can do what you like, but I'm staying,' said *La Vache qui Rit*. 'I don't want to be a cow. There's nothing in this world more stupid than a stupid cow!'

'But how can you say that? *We're* not stupid!' I protested.

'All cows are stupid!' she cried hoarsely. Then she walked straight past me and into the dark cave.

'Be careful!' I warned her, because it looked as if one of the boar was about to attack her, but that isn't what happened. Instead, the boar came closer and began sniffing her, as did the other four. It was clear they were going to welcome her as one of them.

'Listen, my dear,' I heard the voice say. 'Leave this cave. Your friend, alas, is somewhat disturbed and has chosen to take a step back and return to the wild. Don't be too downcast. I know it can be very painful to lose a friend, but there's no emotional pain that can't be cured by walking. So, off you go, my dear. And don't forget to eat, because eating well helps too.'

I left the cave and, very slowly, I set off towards

a wood where the snow appeared to be lying less thickly. I wasn't walking slowly out of obedience to The Pest, but because my friend's decision had drained me of all energy. It was hardly unexpected, but it was still a real blow to see her lying down with those wild boar. As the saying goes:

TASTING AND SWALLOWING ARE TWO
VERY DIFFERENT THINGS.

The winter was nearly at an end, and so I merely sheltered in the hollow of a rock to protect me from the outer cold. It took every ounce of my strength to protect me from the inner cold, though. *La Vache qui Rit* and I had been friends for a long time. And now we were no longer friends, and that made me sad. Not because of loneliness or boredom or anything specific, but simply because I wouldn't see her again. We'd been such good friends and had faced so many dangers together!

Later on, I was bothered by something else too. I kept remembering her last words to me: 'All cows are stupid!'

I couldn't get those words out of my head, and the more I thought about them, the truer they seemed. After all, who was the only intelligent cow I had known? *La Vache qui Rit*, of course, but, as it turned out, she wasn't a cow exactly, but a mixture of wild boar and cow.

From my hollow in the rock, I would sometimes watch the snow falling, and it seemed to me that I was like one of those soft, silly flakes of snow, whereas the wild boar were like vibrant, vigorous hailstones. I was feeling very depressed about my bovine nature. Then The Pest decided to step in.

'We need to talk, my dear,' she said to me one day when spring was nearly upon us. 'Forgive me for saying so, but I think you're overreacting. You haven't left this hollow in the rock for nearly three weeks, and that's not good. You must go forth and eat. The weather is much milder now, and the bitter, fresh young grass that's so full of vitamins is springing up all over the hills.'

I still didn't move. I just didn't feel like it, and I didn't feel like it because I was a cow from head to hoof, and the most stupid thing in this world is a cow, just a cow pure and simple, because 'stupid cow' is a tautology. Not that I wanted to be a wild boar, because I didn't share *La Vache qui Rit*'s views at all, but what about being a horse? Yes, how come I wasn't a horse? Why couldn't I be a horse? And if not a horse, at least a cat… sometimes a crow would come over to me, and I even envied him, I really did, because at least crows can fly. Where would you find a cow that could fly? Nowhere. Further proof that even crows were better than cows.

The sun was growing hotter, and the grass on the hills was growing longer, but still I refused to leave my rock. I simply ate whatever grass was nearby. Finally, The Pest spoke up again, rather angrily this time: 'You're getting thinner by the day, my dear, and I can't allow that. You'll make yourself ill. You're being really stupid.'

'Exactly, because there's nothing in the world more stupid than a cow,' I retorted.

'There are more things in this world, my dear, than you can dream of,' the voice went on very seriously. 'You've always lived among these same few mountains, and so you can't possibly know, but there are many things in the world. And many places too. For example, there are large countries like India and Pakistan, which are worthy of our admiration.'

'Pakistan!' I repeated. I liked the sound of that name.

'Yes, India and Pakistan. And in those great nations do you know which animal they have made into a god, which animal is considered to be the most blessèd, no, the most sacred of beasts?'

'The horse!' I cried.

'Oh, enough about horses, my dear!' The Pest said somewhat tetchily. 'No, the most sacred animal there is the cow,' she went on, more calmly this time. 'They call them *Go*, and you cows are considered to be on the same level as priests. If a cow kneels down in the street, no one will tell her to move, instead, they'll wait until she stands up. And meanwhile, people will touch the cow, then raise one hand to their forehead as a sign of respect. And listen to this: anyone who kills a cow will be hanged.'

'Excellent,' I said, nodding. Everything else seemed a little over-the-top to me, but I liked the idea of cow-killers being hanged. 'Are India and Pakistan very far away?' I asked, remembering the large-toothed twins.

'I'm afraid so, my dear,' said The Pest, guessing my thoughts. 'They're a very long way away. Green Glasses and his assistants will never go there. Switzerland is closer, and cows are pretty important there too, but I don't think they'd go so far as to hang anyone who murdered a cow.'

I said nothing, feeling rather surprised. India, Pakistan and Switzerland were all countries of which I knew nothing, and they were, it would seem, very pleasant places too.

'So there you are, my dear. You were blind and

now you can see. The world doesn't end here, and we cows are in an enviable position. So off you go, my dear, and start showing some common sense. Don't sacrifice your health by neglecting your diet.'

For the first time in ages, I gladly accepted The Pest's advice and headed off to the fields of green grass. Springtime was waiting there, in that lush green grass.

Gradually, as the Wheel of Time continued to turn, spring took over the whole hillside. Grasses and little flowers sprang up everywhere, and I ate my fill of both. Within a couple of weeks, I'd already regained the weight I'd lost over winter, and I then had plenty of time to rest. To rest and to think, of course.

'I like that story about Pakistan, and, as a cow, I feel really proud,' I said to myself one sunny morning.

'Pakistan, India and Switzerland,' The Pest said, correcting me.

'And how have cows fared throughout history?' I asked casually. This was, in fact, a question that had been bothering me since the beginning of spring. 'As far as I know, we don't appear in any cave paintings,' I added. 'Bears do, so do deer and horses, but we don't. Why is that? Were we not considered important in ancient times?'

The Pest took her time before answering, then said: 'In one way, you're right, my dear. We don't appear in the cave paintings, but remember, they were painted when the world was very Alpha. Then things changed. The world began its long journey towards Omega, and then cows were born. In classical Greece, for example. Do you know the story of Troy?'

'No, not yet.'

'All the great Greek heroes fought in that war, Achilles and Patroclus from Athens as well as Ajax from Sparta, and everyone else. They wanted to conquer the city of Troy. However, the years passed, and they couldn't penetrate the city walls. Not even Achilles could. So what did they do? They built a huge wooden cow, the Trojan Cow, and a lot of warriors hid inside it. And what did the Trojans do when they saw this thing?'

'I don't know.'

'Well, they brought it into the city, because they really liked the look of that cow. They thought it was a kind of toy.'

'And then what happened?'

'Well, the war was won, and Troy was conquered, because the warriors inside the wooden cow waited until dark, then emerged from their hiding place, opened the gates of the city and let in their fellow warriors. And that is the story of the Trojan Cow.'

'The Trojan Cow!' I cried. I loved that story and entirely believed it. I now know that it was completely false, but who would have thought The Pest would lie? Such a possibility had never even occurred to me.

Step by step, and with help from The Pest, I became myself again and remained in good spirits until the summer. I would sometimes look over at the thick undergrowth and see six black dots running in a line: the five wild boar and *La Vache qui Rit*, but, by then, I rarely thought about her.

One night, while I was pondering, I suddenly realised that my time living in the hills was over. I had to leave. But where should I go? That was the really difficult part. Ten times I thought of Balanzategui and ten times I rejected the idea. The Wheel of Life cannot turn backwards.

'I'll set off downhill and then I'll see,' I told myself, and the path I took led me to a solitary house, and after that solitary house, the path grew wider and wider and led me to a small settlement. I then followed a road that brought me to a village. It seemed to be a very pretty village, with a stream very similar to the one in Balanzategui, and so I decided I would live there.

The only problem for a cow like me — who had for a long time lived far from the madding crowd — was precisely the lack of any madding crowd, it was far too peaceful. I wanted to see people, chickens, pigs, other cows, whatever; I wanted a little hustle and bustle, children playing, cats jumping from roof to roof, anything; but there was nothing to see or hear. Does anyone live here, I wondered. But someone must live here, I thought, because the fields were well cared for. If it hadn't been for the fenugreek and the clover on which I grazed — at last, after all that time! — on the banks of the little stream, I might have left in search of somewhere livelier. But a cow does not live on liveliness alone, and so I decided to stay close to my food.

One evening, as it was getting dark, I sensed that something was happening in one corner of the village. Yes, a man was singing, and rather well too. A shiver ran through me when I heard him, and I remembered Genoveva and the records she used to play in the living room in Balanzategui. It had been such a long time since I'd heard music! And such a long time since I first heard the sound of a piano! And come to think of it, how would *La Vache qui Rit* be able to put up with living among those wild boar? For as far as I know, wild boar have no interest in music at all...

I drove such thoughts from my mind and went over to the spot where the man was singing — a small mound on which two houses stood side by side. The man was standing beneath the balcony of one of those houses, and was enthusiastically singing a Basque song:

ZÜ ZIRA ZÜ, EKHIAREN PARIA,
LILIAREN FLORIA
ETA MIRAIL EZINAGO GARBIA!
IKHUSIRIK ZURE BEGITARTEA
ELIZATEKE POSIBLE, MAITIA
DÜDAN PAZIENTZIA
HANBAT ZIRADE LORIFIKAGARRIA![1]

He was a very big man, the kind who could effortlessly steer a pair of oxen, and yet out of that burly chest came the sweetest of voices, perhaps infected by the sweetness of that sweet love song. It seemed impossible that such a great hulk of a man could have such a delicate voice.

When he finished his song, he stayed there, gazing up at the balcony, as if expecting someone

1 You are like the sun, you are like the flower, like a crystal-clear mirror. If I were to see your face, I could not possibly be so patient. You are so worthy of praise!

to come out. Indeed, thanks to my broader field of vision, I was able to make out a shadow or a figure behind the curtains. Unfortunately, the shadow gave no sign of coming out onto the balcony, and so the man felt obliged to begin singing again:

ZÜ ZIRA ZÜ, EKHIAREN PARIA,
LILIAREN FLORIA...

But the shadow remained hidden behind the curtains. In the end, after singing the same song five or six times, the man gave up and went into the house next door.

'Well, at least he doesn't have far to go,' I thought.

That scene was repeated each evening, and each evening I was there in the audience, along with the shadow on the balcony. However, even though the big man sang that song with ever more feeling, the shadow still didn't budge. That balcony was like the city of Troy.

'She's certainly elusive!' I thought, looking at the shadow, and then, harking back to former times, I began making bets with myself: I bet the big man will get bored after another three days, not counting today, or else, by next Monday, he'll have thrown a stone at the balcony window.

But the big man was a very patient fellow, and he continued his regular singing sessions, although he did change his song. With more gusto than ever, he sang the song of the eight watermills:

ZAZPI EIHERA BADITUT ERREKA BATEAN,
ZORTZIGARRENA ALDIZ ETXE SAIHETSEAN;
HIRU USO DOAZI KARROSA BATEAN,
HETARIK ERDIKUA ENE BIHOTZEAN.[2]

Eight watermills was a lot of watermills, but that didn't seem to matter to the shadow behind the curtains, which never appeared on the balcony. And so it went on day after day. The patience of the man! In his situation, I would have bellowed and bellowed and woken up everyone in the village. He was different. He made do with singing and gazing up at the balcony.

One day — because as they say, misfortunes never come singly — it began to rain, and the evenings became drab and dreary. The big man took the hint. He again changed his song and dedicated these words to the shadow:

XARMEGARRIA, ZURE BERRIRIK,
NEHONDIK EZ DUT ADITZEN;
NI ZOMBAT GISAZ MALERUSA NAIZEN,

---

2 I have seven water mills in one river, and the eighth next to my house. Three doves ride by in a carriage, of the three, the one in the middle is in my heart.

EZ DUZIA, BA, KONTSIDERATZEN?
ZUTAZ AIPHATZEAK, ADITZEAK BERAK
BIHOTZA DERAUT NIGARREZ URTZEN. [3]

This was a terribly melancholy song, which is perhaps why the shadow behind the curtains vanished. The big man was still singing this song, when, suddenly, a leaf from a nearby tree fluttered to the ground before him. He fell silent. He understood that summer was over. He understood that he could do no more. He understood that sometimes we are left all alone. He then turned and went into his house. The big man's singing sessions had ended for good.

However, a cow is an animal of fixed habits, and so I kept to my usual routine. Each evening, after having eaten my fill of fenugreek and clover, I would take a stroll past that balcony. Unbeknown to me, I was laying the foundations of my future.

It happened one windy evening at the beginning of that same autumn. I was walking along beneath the balcony where the shadow used to hide, when, all of a sudden, something dropped down on top of me. It not only dropped down on top of me, it stayed there, its legs astride my neck.

'Oh, I'm sorry, cow. I didn't know you were

---

3 My beloved, I've had no news from you. Do you not realise how wretched I am? Even the sound of your name makes my heart weep.

there,' said the thing on top of me. It was, of course, the shadow, a very small, very pretty girl, who looked like she would be a dab hand at scything. In other words, it was Pauline Bernadette.

'Why did you throw yourself off the balcony?' I asked.

'I didn't mean to throw myself,' she protested. 'That would be against God's will. No, I jumped because I want to go to the convent. Pierre wants to marry me, my parents want me to marry Pierre, but, I want to go to the convent. That's why I escaped, that's why I am where I am.'

Where she was, of course, was sitting on my back, and she showed no sign of wanting to get off. It was then that I understood how horses must feel.

'He seems to sing quite well,' I said, meaning Pierre.

'Quite well! He's the best singer in Altzürükü and in all of Soule!' she exclaimed. 'And I've told him a thousand times: if you love me, Pierre, study to be a priest and come to the convent to give mass. That way we'll be together for the rest of our lives. But he says that wouldn't be the same thing at all. I don't know why.'

'Nor do I,' I said. Because, after spending so much time up in the hills, I knew very little about life.

'And you, where are you from? You're not one of our cows. And not one of Pierre's either!'

'True. As the poet said, "I am not from here".'

Pauline Bernadette thought for a moment. Then she said:

'I need a dowry in order to enter the convent, and I don't have one. My parents want nothing to do with convents.'

She didn't dare say anything more, but I knew what she meant. I thought to myself: 'I can't go back to Balanzategui. So why not go to the convent? Besides, she really does look like she would be a dab hand at scything!'

'We can go there now if you like,' I said.

'Oh, thank you, Mo, thank you!' she cried.

'How did you know my name?'

'Because I'm a bit of a fortune-teller too, like the saints.'

'She's obviously slightly touched, like *La Vache qui Rit*,' I thought. 'But that seems to be my lot, to be thrown together with people who are not quite logical.'

With that thought in my head, I set off along the road. The following day, we were both happily installed in the convent.

# Ninth Chapter

Here endeth these memoirs, at least for the moment

'Listen, my dear, has not the hour arrived? Is this not the appropriate, correct and most suitable moment?' Thus spake The Pest or The Voice, or whatever that old inner friend of mine is called, on that faraway night of thunder and lightning, before ordering me to write these memoirs, by which she meant that I could not possibly depart this world without leaving my personal testimony.

I began reluctantly at first, and purely so that The Pest would leave me in peace, but I soon began to enjoy writing and remembering, and threw myself into the task heart and soul. I thought it would be a way of lightening my load and that, like the plough turning over the soil, it would bring order and health to my inner life. Line by line, chapter by chapter, it would answer all my questions and reveal the very substance of my life.

Like most things in this world, though, my initial goal turned out to be an illusion, because, however hard you push, the pen can't forge ahead like the plough; it doesn't cut through our memories cleanly and carefully, it does so in a clumsy, disorderly manner, discarding what should be said and bringing to the surface what would have been better left hidden. Do these memoirs reveal the substance of my life? I don't think so. When I re-read what I've written so far, I'm surprised. I haven't talked about the things I intended to talk about, and some of the views expressed don't ring true at all. For example, right at the start, I wrote that, if I could, I would go back to Balanzategui, and I can't imagine anything further from the truth. Go back to Balanzategui? No way! I have a far better life here in the convent with Pauline Bernadette.

The worst thing, though, isn't that the memoirs are full of inexactitudes and lies, which is perhaps true of all memoirs. The worst thing is that remembering and setting down on paper what you remember brings no relief at all. Far from getting fewer in number, the questions only multiply, and leave you feeling still more troubled. If we cows were apples, we would ripen on the branch until we were ready and, at that precise moment — having found answers to all our questions — we would drop to the ground. But we are not apples and will never ripen and never be ready, and when we fall from the branch, we will carry with us all the anxieties of an apple that is still green. As the saying goes:

OLD COWS DIE TOO SOON.

Or put another way: when the Wheel of Time has completed however many or few turns have been allotted to us, our Wheel of Secrets has barely got started. The answers and explanations we once demanded, the mud we hoped to be able to mould in our hands and thus give a shape to the reality of our life, that and many other things will be denied to us.

Re-reading what I've written, my head fills with questions: What will have become of Genoveva? Will they have released her from prison? And will new trees have sprung up in the woods in Balanzategui? Will Green Glasses get his just deserts? And what about *La Vache qui Rit*? Will she still be alive? So many questions — too many — and they're not the only ones. Because, naturally, I have many more. For example: What am I — apart from being a cow? Why am I here? What exactly is the inner voice that speaks to me? Because, even though Pauline Bernadette tells me precisely what the cow Bidani once told me, that the voice is my

217

Guardian Angel, I find this impossible to believe. I sometimes think it's just me, and that I actually have two voices, an inner one and an outer one. Indeed, reading these memoirs, that does seem the most likely explanation. But, of course, there's no way of knowing.

No, remembering and the task of setting down on paper what we remember brings no relief, and doesn't lighten our burden, it only makes it heavier.

'What's wrong with you lately, Mo?' Pauline Bernadette asked me the other day when we were in the convent garden, while she was digging up carrots and I was sampling them.

'You seem so sad,' she added.

'Nothing's wrong, Sister. It's just that I'm getting old. And as that great Basque poet Uztapide once sang:

THE OLD TREE HAS NOTHING, ONLY WITHERED BRANCHES AND DRIED LEAVES.'

'Oh, really, Mo!' she exclaimed, offering me a small carrot. 'You're not old! Remember how briskly you walked along when we set off for Altzürükü the other day. No, that isn't the problem. There's something else on your mind.'

'Yes, you're right,' I said and then I told her

what a frustrating business remembering is, how my memoirs don't tell the whole truth, and how this really worries me. 'That's why I'm a bit low,' I concluded.

'Oh, really, Mo,' she laughed, not even looking up from the row of carrots. 'I know you're a very serious writer, Mo, but not that serious. No, there's something else worrying you.'

Pauline Bernadette and I have been together for many years, and she knows me well, better than anyone. I was unsure whether to tell her the truth or not.

'Come on, Mo, out with it,' she said, leaving her carrots for a moment. She folded her arms and waited.

'Well, the problem is that my inner voice ordered me to remember, to go back over my whole life. "You're getting old and it's time," said the voice. "It's time to write your memoirs," she said. I didn't suspect anything at first, but lately I've come to realise that it was a terrible thing to ask me to do really, because when is it that people usually write their memoirs? When they come to the final bend in the road, that's when. And that's what I'm afraid of, Sister. What will happen the day I finish these memoirs?'

This was the truth. I stood with head bowed.

'And what point in your life have you reached so far in your memoirs, Mo?'

'Our arrival at the convent.'

'Excellent!' she cried, stamping on a carrot. 'It's as clear as day what you have to do: stop writing now. Say nothing about what has happened to you since you came to the convent!'

'But I can't do that, Pauline Bernardette. My inner voice is ordering me to write.'

'Of course, but the voice will want you to write well, and what do you have to do to write well?'

'Oh, everyone knows that.'

'Exactly, Mo, edit, polish, revise! And that's what you should do if you want to obey your inner voice: edit, polish and revise what you've written so far. Do you know how long it took St Augustine to edit, polish and revise his *Confessions*?'

'No, I don't.

'Ten years, Mo, ten years!'

When I heard that, I breathed more easily.

'And what happened then? Did he die?' I asked.

'Certainly not! After spending ten years editing, polishing and revising, he began the second part of his *Confessions*. And now, forgive me, Mo, but I have work to do.'

And the little nun began putting the carrots in her basket. For my part, I felt much easier in my mind. Then I went and knelt down on the lawn of the convent garden and made a decision: I would edit, polish and revise the first part of my life. Then, one day, if necessary, I would continue with the rest. And that's what I've done until now. As the saying goes:

A COW AT LEISURE WILL PUT OFF
EVERYTHING BUT PLEASURE.

### Nobody can stop Don Carlo – Oliver Scherz

Carlo misses his father. His parents are separated, he is with his mother in Germany while his father is back in their native Palermo. His father is always about to visit but somehow never quite gets to Germany. Carlo gets tired of waiting and decides to do something about it and sets off for Palermo but without any money to pay his fare. What happens is a series of adventures when anything that could go wrong does but Carlo despite everything gets to Palermo and lands up at his Papa's door.

This story will strike a chord with many readers as they take Carlo into their hearts.

£7.99   ISBN  978 1 912868 02 5   96p   B. Format

◆◆◆◆◆◆◆

### The Books that devoured my Father – Afonso Cruz

Vivaldo Bonfim was a bored book-keeper whose main escape from the tedium of his work was provided by novels. In the office, he tended to read rather than work, and, one day, became so immersed in a book that he got lost and disappeared completely. That, at least, is the version given to Vivaldo's son, Elias, by his grandmother. One day, Elias sets off, like a modern-day Telemachus, in search of the father he never knew. His journey takes him through the plots of many classic novels, replete with murders, all-consuming passions, wild beasts and other literary perils.

£7.99   ISBN  978 1 912868 04 9   116p   B. Format

### The Girl from the Sea & other stories –
### Sophia de Mello Breyner Andresen

The stories included in this collection are classics of children's literature and have been cherished by generations of Portuguese children. The author is one of Portugal's greatest poets and, like her poetry, these stories are filled with her delight and pleasure in nature, gardens and the sea, as well as her keen sense of the magical. Among other things, we encounter dwarves, diminutive little girls who live on the sea bed, plants that come alive at night, a tree that lives on long after it has been felled, and a pilgrim who discovers much more than the Holy Land.

£11.99   ISBN  978 1 912868 03 2   306p   B. Format

◆◆◆◆◆◆◆

### The Adventures of the Ingenious Alfanhuí –
### Rafael Sánchez Ferlosio

'Trees with feathers for leaves, birds with leaves for feathers, lizards that turn into gold, rivers of blood and transparent horses – these are just some of the magical occurrences in this enchanting fairytale. This book of wild ideas and true lies is a kaleidoscopic celebration of the natural world, and a poetic parable on the passage from innocence to experience.'

Lisa Allardice in *The Independent on Sunday*

£9.99   ISBN  978 1 910213 82 7   199p   B. Format

# Young Dedalus 2020

Nobody can stop
Don Carlo

Oliver Scherz

translated by Deirdre McMahon

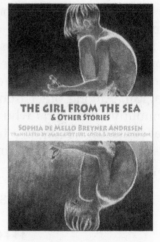

THE GIRL FROM THE SEA
& OTHER STORIES

SOPHIA DE MELLO BREYNER ANDRESEN
TRANSLATED BY MARGARET JULL COSTA & ROBIN PATTERSON

MEMOIRS
OF A
BASQUE COW

Bernardo Atxaga
translated by Margaret Jull Costa

THE BOOKS
THAT
DEVOURED MY FATHER

AFONSO CRUZ
translated by Margaret Jull Costa